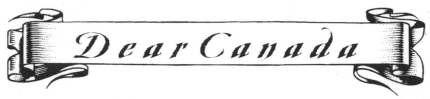

Whispers of War

The War of 1812 Diary of Susanna Merritt

BY KIT PEARSON

Scholastic Canada Ltd.

Niagara Peninsula,
Upper Canada
May, 1812

10 May 1812

This is the best present I have ever received.

Today my beloved brother Hamilton returned from Kingston, where he has been for the past two weeks, selling flour and buying supplies for the farm. I missed him terribly.

What a great many items he unpacked! Coffee and souchong tea, brandy and rum, loaf sugar, salt, a soup tureen and a silver ladle, many tools and a handsome clock for the parlour.

He also brought everyone a present: a volume of Scott's poetry for Mama, tobacco for Papa, velvet ribbons for Maria (how she will preen in front of Charles!) and a handkerchief for Tabitha. She says she will never use it, it is so pretty.

And for me, this elegant little book! It has red leather covers and many thick creamy pages.

"Use it to tell your story, Susanna," said Hamilton, as I thanked him.

"What story?" I asked.

"The story of your life. You are living in a brand new country. Write down what happens to you every day and you will have something interesting to show your grandchildren."

Grandchildren! That is too strange to think about — I am only eleven!

Hamilton has a journal — he writes in it every day, and he has shown me bits. *His* life has been like a story. So have Mama and Papa's, and Tabitha's. Compared with them, Maria and I have led dull lives.

I would rather my life were dull than dangerous, however. Mama and Papa and Tabitha have all experienced terrible wars. Hamilton was once almost shipwrecked, even though he is only nineteen. I would not like to endure what they have.

My safe life will probably not interest my grandchildren. But I do like writing. I enjoy putting my thoughts into words and, until now, I have not had the paper to do so. So I will endeavour to record each day, no matter how humdrum.

Right now I am too sleepy to write much more. We stayed up late to celebrate Hamilton's homecoming. Papa asked Tabitha to bring us some port wine and he offered a glass to her, also. (She became giddy and had to go to bed.) Mama played the pianoforte and Maria and I sang "Come Unto Him," which we learnt while Hamilton was away. My voice squeaked on the high notes, and that annoyed Maria. She never fails to remind me that she is a far better singer than I.

Hamilton showed us a device he bought for himself — a thin piece of wood with bristles set in it, for cleaning his teeth. The rest of us laughed at him — he is always taken by new inventions.

I sneaked Jack into the house and when Papa noticed he did not object as he usually does. "You treat that dog like a person, Susanna," Hamilton said, as I lay with my head on Jack's warm side. I ignored Hamilton's teasing. No one but I understands how Jack dislikes being apart from us.

How thankful I am when the outside world does not intrude upon our family's peace! Tonight, for once, my tears about the future were soothed and I felt safe.

Now the candle is almost out and Maria is grumbling at me to come to bed. So I will end my first entry.

11 May 1812

Dear Granddaughter,

It is easier to think of things to write about if I imagine a grandchild reading them. I hope she is a girl, as I do not care for boys. Here is what happened today, my faraway granddaughter. It was much like any other day, except for the end of it.

I was up in time to kiss Papa goodbye before he left for Niagara. The house will seem empty until he returns next Sunday. But at least Hamilton is back. It was reassuring to see him as usual in the barn, milking the cows while I gathered the eggs.

We sat at breakfast together. Tabitha poached us some whitefish. When Hamilton told me I had butter on my face, I pinched his ear and he chased me all over the kitchen.

Tabitha said that dear Mama had a headache. I took her up a cup of marjoram tea and we said morning prayers together before I left for school. Maria was still in bed. She is lazy, and I told her so before I went downstairs.

It was a glorious morning, sunny and warm. Chickadees called to each other noisily. A bluebird was sitting in a cherry tree — the plumage of its red breast was brilliant against the white blossoms and the blue sky. Hamilton helped me catch Sukie, who is getting more bad-tempered and stubborn every day.

I suppose I had better tell you who are the people and animals I write about. Sukie is my pony, who was given to me on my seventh birthday. Papa called her the nickname I had as a little child, much to my dismay — sometimes the boys at school call me Sukie to taunt me.

I had to kick Sukie's sides to get her to start moving. How I wish I had a real horse! But Papa says I am not big enough. It is frustrating to be so small for my age — I hardly seem to grow at all.

The wide creek sparkled in the morning sun and a pair of hawks circled high above the mountain. Jack followed me for a while until I shooed him home. Sukie agreed to trot once she realized she could not turn back, and I quickly reached the Seabrooks' farm.

Abbie Seabrook has only lived at the Twelve for two years — she and her parents and two little brothers came here from Connecticut. She is my closest friend, the first real friend I have ever had, since the other girls near our farm are not my age. Abbie's father is still clearing their land and their log house is small and dark compared to our large frame one.

Mr. Seabrook frowned at me as Abbie climbed on to Sukie's back. He does not approve of Abbie attending school — he thinks she should be staying home to help. Her mother, however, has never learned to read and write and wishes Abbie to do so.

Papa does not like Abbie's father, or any of the many Americans who have moved here during the last few years. Mr. Seabrook is much younger than my father. *His* father was on the opposite side to Papa during the Revolutionary War. "That war is long over, Thomas," Mama says. "The Seabrooks have as much right to be here as we do."

When the Seabrooks first came, Mama called on them. But now Papa discourages her from visiting Mrs. Seabrook. At first he objected also to my friendship with Abbie. Mama reminded him that we were only children, and that I needed a friend. Papa, who has always doted on me, relented.

Abbie and I chattered all the way to school. I told her about the presents Hamilton had brought and she complained, as usual, about her mischievous brothers. I like having Abbie's warm body perched behind me. When I used to ride alone I was quite frightened of the thick, dark forest, but now that I have a companion I am not.

Our school is as small and dark as Abbie's house, and in the winter we all have to bring wood to keep it warm. The only other buildings in the village are the church, the inn, the store and a warehouse, with the mills in the valley below. When Mama and Papa came here sixteen years ago, there were not even those.

Our village is much smaller than Niagara — so small that it goes by several names. Some call it "Shipman's Corners," some "Twelve-Mile Creek" or "St. Catharines." My family has always called it "the Twelve."

There are only four girls in our school, counting Abbie and me. The other eleven scholars are all boys. What a difficult time they give us! As I was bending over to tie up Sukie, Elias Adams sneaked up and thrust a worm down the back of my neck.

It felt unpleasantly slimy but I pretended it did not bother me and walked, I hope, coolly away to the privy to get it free.

Elias is a troublesome boy. He never leaves me alone, and because our fathers are good friends I have to pretend to be civil to him at social gatherings.

School was as usual. I am afraid Mr. Simmons is a very poor teacher. (I have learnt far more from Mama.) He spends most of his time reading his newspaper behind the desk while we write long tedious lists by rote on our slates. Today it was all the dates of the British monarchies. I do enjoy handwriting, however, and I made my list as neat as possible.

Nathaniel and Caleb were whipped for having a fistfight at dinnertime. I do not like it when the boys fight, but I also do not like watching them being whipped. I averted my eyes and drew a picture on my slate of Jack wearing a hat. Abbie laughed when I passed it to her.

I am proud to be the first girl in our family to go to school. Caroline and Maria learnt their lessons from Mama. (Maria did not learn very much, I am sorry to say.) Mama intended to teach me at home as she did my sisters, but when she was ill with dropsy I was allowed to start school. I enjoyed it so much she did not have the heart to take me out of it, although she is disappointed in Mr. Simmons's teaching.

Mama herself attended a girls' school in South Carolina. She says I need to learn more drawing and French and dancing — therefore, next year I am to attend the new female academy in Niagara. I shall have to live there during the week, since Niagara is twelve miles from here. I know that Mama wishes me to have as refined an education as she did, but I dread being away from my family and from Abbie.

I wanted Abbie to come and see this journal, but when we stopped at her house her mother made her stay and do chores. So I went home and helped Tabitha get supper. Hamilton had shot a porcupine and we roasted it — it was delicious. With it we had potatoes and turnips and applesauce. I always try to eat a lot so I will grow.

Every evening after supper I sit on my stool in the parlour with the rest of the family until we all retire. Tonight Mama and Maria and I sewed while Hamilton told us more stories about

Kingston. Then he brought up the subject I dread. "Everyone in Kingston believes there will be a war," he said.

Mama covered her eyes, even though her headache had gone. "Pray that there is not," she said. "Oh, please pray that there is not! We have had too much war. I cannot bear the thought of another."

My heart leapt in my throat. All my life, it seems, I have sat on my stool and listened to the adults talk about war. Mama's older brother, Richard, fought in Papa's regiment against the Rebels and was killed by them in Virginia. Mama was as devoted to Richard as I am to Hamilton. She often tells me about the terrible day when she found out he was dead.

Papa has also told me about his brother, Shubal, who was shot by some Whigs who had a personal quarrel with him, when he returned to New York from New Brunswick after the war. Two uncles I will never know, all because of the war.

Mama began to weep, and Hamilton soothed her by reading poems from the book he had brought her. I leaned against her and no one knew how violently my heart was beating.

Will there really be a war? The adults have been talking about it for months, but I do not entirely understand it. There has been a war between France and Britain for years, of course. Hamilton has tried to explain to me that now there is a quarrel between Britain and the United States. It has something to do with Britain blockading American vessels at sea. Because Upper Canada belongs to Britain, we may have to be part of the conflict. Hamilton calls Britain "the Lion" and the United States "the Eagle." Poor little Upper Canada could become their prey, like a mouse being torn apart by two fierce animals.

When I think of war I feel the same icy dread as when Mama talks about her brother Richard. What if *my* brother had to fight? Perhaps Papa would as well, although I hope he would be considered too old.

I cannot bear the prospect. I will do as Mama asks and pray tonight that God will spare us such a calamity.

It comforts me to be able to tell you my fears, Granddaughter. What a great many pages I have written! I know I should not boast, but the black ink of my handwriting does look distinctive on these white pages.

"Come to bed, Susanna," says Maria. All she wants to do is talk about Charles.

Dear Constance,

Do you like the name I have given you? It makes you seem more real. I wonder what you are like. I imagine you are my age. And I have decided that you are my *great*-granddaughter. That way I will probably not be alive when you read this. It will encourage me to make my life as vivid as possible to you.

Last night I cried out so much in my sleep that Maria had to shake me awake. But today has been so normal that I have managed to push down my fears of war. At school, since I finished my work so quickly, Mr. Simmons asked me to listen to the three little ones, George, Sarah and Timothy, recite their lessons. I greatly enjoyed doing this and they later impressed Mr. Simmons with how much I had taught them.

At dinnertime I ate with Abbie, Elizabeth and Sarah as usual. Elias, Henrik, Timothy and Uriah hovered around us and drove us to distraction with their teasing. Uriah called Abbie a speckled hen (Abbie has many freckles) and Elias kept saying, "Here Sukie, Sukie, Sukie," as if he were calling a pig. Finally I led the other girls into the school, where we latched the door against the boys and continued our meal. They pounded and pounded to no avail.

When Mr. Simmons returned — he goes to the inn for his dinner — he wanted to know why we were inside, which is not permitted when he is away. I explained that the boys would give us no peace. I feared he would be angry, but he smiled and said that we could come inside when we needed to.

Mr. Simmons is a kind man, despite being a poor teacher. All afternoon he had us add up long lists of numbers while he snored behind his desk. There was so much rum on his breath that the boys held their noses, but no one dared laugh aloud.

Abbie told me some discouraging news. Her mother has just learned she is expecting another child, so this will be Abbie's last term at school. I fear she will never attend again. I promised to lend her books next fall and, when I am home from Niagara each week's end, to teach her what I have learnt. This cheered her considerably.

When I reached home Hamilton and I rode his horse all over our land to inspect the crops. The corn and rye and barley are already poking up through the ground and the wheat Hamilton planted in the fall is quite high. We saw a doe with a fawn so young it could barely totter.

Hamilton's horse is very handsome, a tall black stallion called Caesar. How pleasant it was to sit up so high! I asked Hamilton if he thought Papa would give me a horse for my birthday. He reminded me that it is still five months away and asked if I thought I could grow by then.

I told him I would try, which made him laugh. I cannot make myself grow, of course — only God can. So I will begin to pray for that, as well as praying that there will not be a war.

13 May 1812

Dear Constance,

Nothing particularly interesting happened to me today, so tonight I will tell you about the rest of my household.

I will start with my parents. My father, Thomas Merritt, is from New York State. During the Revolutionary War he fought bravely for the King in Colonel Simcoe's regiment. My mother, Mary (but Papa calls her Polly), is from South Carolina. After they married, my parents followed their parents to New Brunswick, along with many other Loyalists. But Mama did not like the climate and in 1785 they returned to New York for a time. There my eldest sister, Caroline, and then Hamilton, were born.

Colonel Simcoe was appointed Governor of Upper Canada. Papa decided that he would rather live under the British government than in a republic, so he, Mama, Caroline and Hamilton (Hamilton was only three years old!) made the long, arduous journey here, where Colonel Simcoe granted him some land.

Mama did not want to come, but of course she had to accompany her husband. She often tells me how difficult it was at first. They were lucky to move into a house already built, but she had never done her own cooking and housekeeping. One day a neighbour found her in tears because she did not know how to bake bread! I tease her about this — I have known how to make bread since I was very young.

Maria and I were both born in Upper Canada, Maria in 1797 and I in 1800. Last year my sister Caroline married James Gordon and moved with him to Burlington Bay. This fall they are to have a child and I will be an aunt!

My parents left a fine house and could only bring with them what they could carry. Mama often tells me how much she misses the United States. She especially longs for her younger sister, Isabel, who still lives in South Carolina.

Papa was appointed Sheriff of Niagara and spends all week there. Mama has slowly made our house comfortable and can now bake and churn and keep everything in order as well as our neighbours do.

Of course she has Tabitha to help her. Tabitha came to us when I was eight, from a place called Norfolk, in England. After she was orphaned, she went to work for a family in England. She made the long sea voyage here with them, but they mistreated her and she was very glad to leave them and come to us. She has a heavy accent that people have trouble understanding, but I am used to it. Tabitha is stout, with rosy cheeks, and she makes me laugh with her stories and songs — except when she talks about the war against France, where her father and brother were killed.

My candle is sputtering and I forgot to bring another one upstairs. So I will tell you about Hamilton's past later and end this entry with a few words about family romances!

Hamilton is deeply in love with Miss Catherine Prendergast, whose father is a doctor here. She is a very handsome girl who frustrates Hamilton terribly because she has neither accepted nor rejected his advances.

Maria is totally besotted with Hamilton's friend, Charles Ingersoll, who lives in Queenston. Whenever he visits she is constantly asking me if I think he is fond of her.

Even Tabitha has a suitor — she has several times been called upon by Samuel Gower, the

Turneys' hired hand. Tabitha is five and thirty, so this could be her last chance to be married. But she is as particular as Catherine and has not given Samuel much encouragement.

As for me, I think all love talk very silly and intend never to marry at all. I will live on this farm all my life and have many horses and perhaps run a school for girls — no boys!

14 May 1812

Dear Constance,

It occurs to me that, if I want a great-grand-child to read this, I will *have* to marry! I hope it is to a boy who is less aggravating than Elias. Today at school we were playing iron tag at dinnertime. I was running so fast to touch the ring where Mr. Simmons ties his horse that my bonnet fell off. Elias grabbed it and threw it into a tree. I had to climb up to get it and ripped my dress, which Mama scolded me about when I got home.

Here is a counting out rhyme that Abbie taught us:

Onery, uery, ickory, a,
Hallibone, crackabone, ninery-lay,
Whisko, bango, poker my stick,
Mejoliky one leg!

Abbie learnt this in Connecticut and I find it very amusing. I repeated it so much to Tabitha in the kitchen tonight that she finally ordered me to hold my tongue.

Now I will continue to tell you about my household. Hamilton has had just as exciting a life as Mama and Papa. At age fifteen he had a great adventure. He set out for New Brunswick, where my grandfather lives, to attend school, but on the way joined our uncle on the crew of a ship that ended up sailing to the Bermudas! On the return journey the ship was almost destroyed in a great storm — Hamilton has often told me how he came close to being swept overboard by the enormous waves.

After that my brother spent time in Saint John and New York and did not come home for a long time. I shall never forget him walking into Christmas dinner as a surprise. I had not seen him for two years, and I clung to his leg so hard he had to pry me off.

For a short while Hamilton ran the store in the Twelve, but he soon gave that up to take care of the farm, Papa being so busy in Niagara. I do not think Hamilton likes farming, however. He is so restless, I sometimes fear he will leave again.

Who else can I tell you about? Ben comes every day to help Hamilton, but I do not know him very well. And of course there are many animals. We have cows, horses, pigs, chickens and barnyard cats. We used to have sheep, but wolves ravaged them last year. And then of course there is my handsome Jack, so noble looking with his white coat and large head.

Those are the persons and animals in my life, Constance. They are all so dear to me. I could not bear it if anything happened to them.

When I went in to kiss Mama goodnight I told her how frightened I was of a war. She told me I was too fanciful, that I should not torture myself with imagining what *could* happen, but should put my trust in God to keep us safe. So I will attempt to do that.

15 May 1812

Dear Constance,

As I was riding back from Abbie's through the darkest part of the forest I met a wolf! It was large and grey and trotted towards me. Sukie froze and would not go on, no matter how much I kicked her sides. The wolf paused and looked intently at us with its narrow golden eyes, as if it were gathering its strength to leap. Then it ran off the trail into the trees.

We often hear wolves howling at night, but I

have never before seen one in the daytime. After
it left I sat for a long time on Sukie's back, both
of us trembling violently. What if it had attacked
us? I stroked Sukie and tried to calm her — to
calm both of us. Mixed with my fear was awe at
the animal's stateliness, and an enormous relief
at being spared. When we had both stopped
shaking we galloped home as fast as we could.

16 May 1812

Dear Constance,

I am writing this before breakfast. I had a
nightmare that the wolf had me pinned under it
and was about to devour me. Just as its gaping
red mouth and huge teeth were descending I
awoke, gasping for air.

I got up and sat by the window, calmed by the
jubilant bird song outside. When Maria began to
stir I asked her if she thought there was going to
be a war.

"How would I know that, Susanna?" she
snapped. Maria is always irritable in the morn-
ings. But when she saw how frightened I was she
told me not to worry, that the men would keep us
safe no matter what happened.

But who will keep the men safe?

Later

The busyness of the day dispelled my fears. We spent the morning sowing the vegetable garden. Mama let me write the labels for each row and I was proud of how neat they looked. We also planted snapdragons, heart's ease, sneezewort and sunflowers in the front yard. Everything is green and budding and summer seems on its way.

I made a scarecrow out of Hamilton's and Papa's old clothes to keep the birds from the garden. I think it looks very realistic.

In the afternoon, after I had done my sewing, I rode to Abbie's. I hoped she could come out, but she had to help her mother spin flax. I helped also, tying the bundles of thread into hanks. It was like magic, watching Mrs. Seabrook pull the white flax into linen thread. We do not spin at home, as we buy all our cloth.

As we worked, Abbie's little brothers, Paul and Johnny, played at our feet. They were very amusing, pretending some sticks of wood were soldiers. Sometimes I wish I had a little brother or sister, but Mama is too old to have another child.

Abbie's house is only one large room, with a loft upstairs where they all sleep. They have to ascend by a ladder. Mrs. Seabrook is shy and does not speak to me much. She does not yet look as if she is with child. Johnny, who is two, was a sweet baby when the Seabrooks moved here.

It will be very agreeable to have another baby to play with. I told this to Abbie and she retorted that she is weary of looking after little brothers and does not look forward to this one.

"Maybe it will be a girl," I told her.

"Even if it is, she will still be a lot of trouble," said Abbie. She was so out of spirits that I went home. Sometimes Abbie seems very different from me.

17 May 1812

Dear Constance,

Today being Sunday, I gave my teeth their weekly cleaning. I was in the kitchen mixing powdered charcoal with honey when Hamilton appeared and dipped his new tooth cleaning brush into it. How I teased him as he moved the brush vigorously around his mouth! Although, I must admit, it seemed less messy than using a flannel.

Then I brushed Jack in the yard. He stood so patiently as I worked through the tangles in his long fur. I brought out the rest of my sausage to him as a reward.

There was no church, as there is not anyone to lead it this week. So Papa read us the service in the parlour. After dinner — a fine one of venison and custard pie — we drove to the Adamses' for a visit. The weather was so warm I borrowed a very pretty parasol of Maria's. At first Mama said I was too young to use a parasol, but then she relented and let me take it. How proud I felt, holding it over my head as Mama and Maria do!

We had an agreeable visit except for the end of it, which I will relate shortly. While the men inspected a new pair of oxen, Mrs. Adams showed us the handsome desk she has just had delivered from New York. Then we all sat down to tea. Elias tried to talk to me but I ignored him and listened to his older sister tell us about her trip to the Falls. I have never been there, and her description of their magnificence gave me a great desire to see them one day.

When we were ready to leave the disaster happened. I opened up my parasol and molasses dripped all over me! Elias had smeared the spokes with it as a trick. While Mrs. Adams and Mama wiped me off, Mr. Adams took Elias out to the back and beat him. I have to confess that I was not sorry I could hear his yells of pain.

I suppose I should have been friendlier to Elias today and he would not have done it. But why should I be civil when he plagues me so at school? Now Maria's parasol is ruined and she is cross with me.

18 May 1812

Dear Constance,

We have started a grand game at school that Conrad thought of — Noah's Ark. We are constructing an ark out of fallen branches and some pieces of lumber we found at the back of the school. Tomorrow Elias and Henrik are going to bring some rope to hold it together.

19 May 1812

Dear Constance,

We have made great progress on our ark. Even Nathaniel, who just turned fourteen, is helping. We have leaned the lumber against ropes tied to tree trunks. Tomorrow we are all going to school early to finish laying pine boughs for a roof.

This pastime is so absorbing that it consumes all my thoughts. At supper Hamilton laughed because I sprinkled sugar, instead of salt, on my meat.

Dear Constance,

Our ark being finished, we spent all dinner hour deciding on our parts. Conrad said that, as it was his idea, he would be God. Uriah is Noah and Abbie is his wife. The rest of us are animals. Of course there are not enough of us to have two of everything, so we are each one animal and have an imaginary mate — except for Elias and Ralph, who are both lions. Here is a list of the other animals:

Sarah: rabbit
Elizabeth: mouse
George: snake
Robert: wolf
Caleb: buffalo
Timothy: eagle
Patrick: elephant
Henrik: whale
Nathaniel: bear

I am a tiger and greatly enjoyed roaring at everyone. Tonight I was growling and clawing at Maria as she was washing. She got very annoyed and told me I was acting like a little child. I do not care what she says.

Dear Constance,

We had such a pleasant dinner hour acting out our story for the first time. Conrad made an impressive God, as he stood on a stump and warned Noah about the Flood. We crawled on our hands and knees into the ark (I tore my dress again and Mama was very displeased). Then we screamed in terror as the waters rose up. We turned little Sarah temporarily into a dove. When she returned with a branch in her mouth I felt as relieved as if we were really in the ark.

We were so absorbed in our game that Mr. Simmons had to ring the bell extra loud to make us come inside. It is a wonder that we are all getting along so well in this game. Even Elias has been pleasant to me, although we roar loudly at each other.

22 May 1812

Dear Constance,

The weather continuing so fine, Mr. Simmons let us take the whole afternoon off to play our game again. He brought his chair outside and watched. We were so noisy that some men at the inn stopped by to observe us. I have almost lost my voice from roaring.

When we finished Mr. Simmons clapped loudly. Then he said something that has brought back my fears. "Play while you can, children," he said sadly. "Play while you still can."

In the Bible God promised Noah that there will never be another Flood. Tonight I shall pray to Him to keep His promise.

23 May 1812

Dear Constance,

Papa is home for a few days and he and Mama spent all day at the Turneys' barn raising. I could not go because I have a bad cold. I was very disappointed. Abbie and I had been planning for a long time how we would wear our best muslins and watch the dancing after the work is done.

Tabitha gave me a hot bath in the kitchen. Then she tucked me into bed and told me stories she had heard from her mother long ago. "Jack the Giant Killer" and "Cinderella" are my favourites. Mama does not approve of fairy tales — she says they are too fanciful and will frighten me. But I find them very satisfying. I always beg Tabitha to tell them to me when we are alone.

The brandy she had given me made me close my eyes. Tabitha sang the lullaby she used to croon when I was younger:

Baby, baby, naughty baby,
Hush, you squalling thing, I say.
Peace this moment, peace, or maybe
Bonaparte will pass this way.

Baby, baby, if he hears you,
As he gallops past the house,
Limb from limb at once he'll tear you,
Just as pussy tears a mouse.

Mama would disapprove of this even more than fairy tales if she knew of it! But I enjoy the prickles it gives me. Napoleon Bonaparte is frightening, of course. He is the wickedest man in the world. But he is far away in France and cannot ever hurt me. He seems just as unreal as Jack the Giant Killer.

The stories I do not like to hear are those Tabitha relates to me about the war against Napoleon that destroyed her whole family. Her father and brother were killed in the Battle of Trafalgar. Having no men to earn wages forced the rest of Tabitha's family into the poorhouse. There her mother and sisters died of putrid fevers — excruciatingly slow and painful deaths, while poor Tabitha nursed them. "Agnes was never strong, but it was losing my father, and especially my brother Tom, which helped killed my mother," Tabitha says. "How we all doted on him!"

When Tabitha tells me this, her eyes welling with tears, I want her to stop. She seems to draw comfort from her memories, however, so I cannot ask her to.

It is like listening to Mama talk about my Uncle Richard or Papa talk about my Uncle Shubal. The older I become, the more I am aware of all the tragedy in the world. Why does God allow it?

I woke up several hours later and felt slightly better. I sat up in bed and had some bread and milk, then I wrote in here. Soon the others will be home and I will try not to be envious of what I have missed.

26 May 1812

Dear Constance,

I got better rapidly but I have not written for a few days because my pen wore down. Hamilton has not had time to cut me a new one. But today he did, just in time to tell you some exciting news.

I am allowed to miss school and go to the King's birthday celebrations and the muster of troops in Niagara with the rest of the family! I am thrilled that I am not to be left behind with Tabitha. Mama says it is to make up for my having to miss the barn raising.

It will be Maria's first ball. Mama thinks she should wait another year, but Maria entreated her so persistently to attend that Mama gave in. For weeks she and Mama have been making her a new dress. It is gauze with a sarcanet underdress, trimmed with embroidered flowers that are the finest Maria has ever sewn. It has a small train. She will look so elegant.

Tonight Maria and I practised our courtesies. Hamilton pretended to be a British officer and we had to courtsy deeply as Mama introduced him to us. I tried not to laugh as Hamilton bowed to me as if I were a lady. Now that Caroline has married, Maria is "Miss Merritt" — how proud she is of that! I am still "Miss Susanna Merritt."

Some day I, too, will attend a ball. How difficult that is to imagine! I do wish I were as handsome as Maria. My face is so white and thin, not rosy and plump like hers. My hair is wispy and dull, while Maria's is thick and glossy. But it is vain to worry about my looks. Mama says it is what is inside that counts.

Of course all Maria has been talking to me about is whether Charles will be at the ball. I hope for my sake he is, or there will no comforting her.

This morning when I was in the barn I overheard Hamilton and Ben talking about what would happen to the animals if there was a war. They sounded so worried that I ran out and dropped two eggs.

Surely we would not be going to Niagara if a war was imminent, would we? I am afraid to ask anyone this.

I missed writing to you, Constance. I like the order it gives to the day, to sum it up in here.

27 May 1812

Dear Constance,

I am in very low spirits — Abbie and I have just had our first quarrel. She told me that, ever since she played being his wife, she has been fond of Uriah. I replied that she is much too young to have such feelings. She reminded me that she is a whole year older than I.

"You are still only twelve!" I cried. "It is not suitable to talk about such things until you are older."

"I can talk about whatever I wish!" Abbie retorted. "I wish I had not told *you*, however, since you are obviously too young to understand."

"Perhaps I should leave, then," I said, as coldly as I could. She did not reply and turned her back on me, so I untied Sukie and rode away. I wept all the way home.

How dare she act so superior! And how can she have such feelings for Uriah? He is just a boy, a dull one who calls her names.

The evening was so fine I sat outside on the swing Papa made me years ago, watching the swallows swoop over the field, and mulling over our quarrel. Jack was beside me, biting at his paws. When I examined him I discovered many burrs imbedded in his fur. I was busy pulling them out when I heard voices. Tabitha and Samuel were walking in the orchard. I kept very still so they would not discover me. I saw Samuel kiss Tabitha!

Does this mean they are betrothed? I hope not, for then Tabitha might leave us.

I am weary of all this love-making. Hamilton visits Catherine every day. Maria goes on so about Charles that I write in here until she falls asleep, to avoid her confidences. And now Abbie is succumbing to this silliness. I promise you, Constance, that I will *never* be like this.

Dear Constance,

I did not call on Abbie on the way to school and we did not speak all day. At dinner she took Sarah and Elizabeth for a walk to pick wildflowers. I was left to watch the boys have a battle between the French and the English.

How tedious are their games of war! All they do is brandish sticks and yell at each other. I suggested that we play Noah's Ark again. "That is a girls' game," said Elias. How could he forget how harmonious we were, and how much he enjoyed being a lion?

"Besides, we have to practise fighting in case there is a real war," said Nathaniel.

I told him he and the others were too young to fight. "Leave us alone, Sukie," said Elias. "You do not understand."

I marched away angrily. Boys are the unpleasantest creatures alive!

My stomach churns with sadness and I could not eat my supper. Mama gave me some castor oil, but that will not cure my quarrel with Abbie. I would have liked to ask Mama's advice, but Catherine and her parents called by and everyone was busy entertaining them in the parlour. I escaped up here to write. I can hear them laughing below and wish so much I could share in their cheerfulness.

29 May 1812

Dear Constance,

Abbie and I are friends again! I am so relieved. This morning before school I went to Mama in her room and told her about our quarrel. She said that I cannot change how another person feels, even if I disagree with her. "Why not apologize?" she suggested.

"She should apologize to *me* for what she said!" I told her. Mama said that it did not matter who apologized first, but if no one did we could lose our friendship. "Is that not valuable to you?" she asked me. That made me weep. Then we prayed together that I could conquer my anger.

I rode to Abbie's house, rehearsing an apology all the way but not sure I could get out the words. Abbie was waiting at the top of her road! As soon as I approached she called out that she was sorry. I jumped down from Sukie and we embraced.

Abbie says she cannot help her feelings for Uriah, but that she will be careful not to talk about them in front of me. All I can do is accept that, and pretend she is the same as before. But I do wish people would not change.

Dear Constance,

This morning poor Jack got tangled with a porcupine and came home with his nose full of quills. Hamilton had to pull them out and I could not bear Jack's whimpers of pain. I let him lie in front of the kitchen fire and cradled his poor tender muzzle. This has happened to him several times before. Why does he not learn?

Tonight Mama told us how, during the Revolutionary War, she and her mother and sister were looted by a band of Patriots. The soldiers did not harm them, but took away all their grain. "One of them was our former neighbour, young Silas," said Mama. "He could not meet my eyes — he knew how hungry we would be without being able to make bread. Isabel was so frightened that she hid in the root cellar the whole time."

I was so frightened to hear this that I changed the subject by asking Mama to remind me about Isabel's family. She is married to a man called Henry Grierson and has three daughters. Annie, the youngest, is very sickly. "I have not heard from Isabel for so long," sighed Mama. "I hope her little Annie is still alive."

It is strange to think that I have relatives in

the United States that I have never met. Emily, the eldest daughter, is my age. I wonder what she is like?

31 May 1812

Dear Constance,
   Maria's dress is finished and she looked so pretty when she tried it on this evening. I helped her lace her stays. Mama told us that stays were much more constricting in her youth. How thankful I am that I do not yet have to wear such a garment!

1 June 1812

Dear Constance,
   Only one more day until we go to Niagara! Abbie is very envious. Her father will be mustering there with his unit — he is too busy to go, but if he does not attend he has to pay a fine. I wish he would take Abbie, but she has to stay home. This afternoon we were helping her mother make bread when Mr. Seabrook came in from the forest for a drink of water. He was covered in bits of bark from head to foot.
   Abbie says her father is a kind man, but he frightens me. He has very dark eyebrows that meet in the middle and make him look menacing.

He never smiles and I do not think he likes me — perhaps he knows how Papa feels about him.

He asked me gruffly why I was always allowed to ride over here by myself. He said that my parents were too indulgent. I wanted to answer that it was only a mile, but of course I could not be rude. "Leave her, Adam," Mrs. Seabrook told him.

After he left Mrs. Seabrook forgot her usual reserve and apologized for her husband. She told me how hard he worked, that he was desperately trying to clear enough land for more crops. They only have one planting of wheat so far, in a field that is still dotted with stumps. That will have to do them all this winter.

"And if there is a war he will have to participate," she said. "Why should he have to fight against our former country?" Her voice quavered and she looked as if she might cry.

I have been so excited about going to Niagara that I forgot to worry about war. Now my fear pounced back, like the wolf in my dream. Abbie looked as frightened as I. Mrs. Seabrook collected herself. "Let us not talk about war," she said. "Perhaps there will not be one." Is there a chance that she could be right? How I hope so!

Tonight I am trying to let that hope grow. I am also reflecting upon Mr. Seabrook's comment. Am I too indulged? I have never considered this before. I am certainly allowed far more freedom than Abbie. She is not allowed to see me on Sundays, or to ever read novels, or to come to my home by herself. And of course she has much more work to do than I. So I *am* indulged, but perhaps that is simply because I am the youngest. I do not see the harm in it.

2 June 1812

Dear Constance,

I stayed home from school to help get ready for Niagara. We have washed and brushed our best clothes, and our boxes are packed and waiting downstairs. Tabitha has given me some money to buy her a looking glass. Is she becoming vain? She has not said anything about herself and Samuel, so perhaps they are not betrothed after all.

The rain is pounding down outside — I do hope it ends in time for our journey. I will stop writing now, Constance, and pack this journal so I can tell you all about it. I am so excited I do not know how I will sleep.

Dear Constance,

We are here, at Papa's house in Niagara! I am writing this early Thursday morning, since I was too tired to last night. The rain cleared and Wednesday was a fine, breezy day. The wagon was crowded with Mama, Hamilton, Maria, myself, our boxes and several barrels of salted pork Hamilton was going to sell.

The road was even rougher than usual, and very soft from the rain. Several times we all had to get out to lighten the load when the horses got stuck. It took us four hours to get here, and our clothes were caked with mud.

What a fine town Niagara is! I was so excited to see it again. I have not been here since January, when we came by sleigh — which of course was much faster — and everything was blanketed in snow.

Before we reached the town we spotted the lighthouse, then the two church spires. The vast blue lake seems to spread out forever. The many elegant houses and stores are of frame or brick, and they stand close together in neat rows. Most have bright gardens in front.

Papa's brick house is right next to Government House. He was given it furnished when he became Sheriff, and it contains many fine pieces that Mama wishes she had at home.

Hannah, the old housekeeper who looks after Papa, is ill-tempered. She never likes it when we are here and complains of the extra work, even though we help her as much as we can.

After we had washed and changed and had dinner, Mama, Maria and I walked up and down the main street and looked at the stores. There was even more to admire than on my previous visits.

Mama gave me two whole shillings to spend! I bought a pair of quills and a paper of ink powder, and I had twopence left over. Maria teased me for spending my money on writing materials instead of frivolities. She herself got a pretty fan for the ball. Mama bought needles, muslin and cambric, mustard, candlesticks and a copper pot. She also purchased some spectacles to help her reading, and we persuaded her to buy some kid leather gloves she was admiring. I found a looking glass that was slightly over the amount Tabitha had given me, but I added my twopence to make it even.

Crowds of people strolled or rode up and down the street, all here for the ball. There were many British soldiers in handsome red coats and snowy breeches, their brass and silver glittering in the sun and their tall hats resplendent with red and white feathers. I do not know how they walk without tripping over their long swords — indeed, a soldier near us almost caught Mama's dress with his, for which he apologized profusely. Several Indians were also on the streets, as splendidly attired as the soldiers. Fine carriages with even finer horses passed us and I gazed so avidly at them that Mama had to remind me not to stare.

We stopped often to chat to someone we knew. Maria met Miss Dickson, who said that Charles *would* be at the ball. Now there is no containing her excitement.

In town supper is eaten much later than at home. Caroline's husband, James, joined us. Mama was very disappointed that Caroline was not well enough to come with him. James is distant with me, as if I were not important. He does not feel like a brother.

The adults were talking about Major General Brock, who lives just next door in Government House when he is in town. He is arriving tomorrow from York. I have heard them talk about General Brock before. He is the President of Upper Canada, and Papa and Hamilton admire him greatly.

"He has had much experience in war and is just as gallant as Colonel Simcoe," said Papa. That is high praise indeed, for Colonel Simcoe is Papa's hero.

Hamilton related how effectively General Brock had quelled a mutiny in his regiment a few years ago. "He is a born leader and commands much respect," he said.

"And I have heard how handsome and charming he is!" said Maria. Mama told her she was much too young to make such a comment.

I was so full of the busy day that soon I could not attend properly to the conversation. I fell asleep in my chair and Papa carried me up to bed.

Later

While everyone else gets ready for the ball I will tell you about today, which has been even more interesting than yesterday! After breakfast Hamilton, Mama and Maria went to call on some friends. Papa had some business at Fort George, so he took me with him. It is only a mile from the town. On the way many people stopped and talked to us and I felt proud holding the hand of my distinguished father. There were a great many Indians camped on the plain between the town and the fort, the men dressed as handsomely as they were yesterday.

Papa had intended to deliver some letters and leave, but when we got to Fort George he was asked to stay for a militia meeting. "What am I to do about *you?*" Papa asked me. He did not want to leave me without a chaperone, but it would not have been suitable for me to attend the meeting. He decided I was to wait on a bench under a tree, and told me not to move from it until he returned.

I grew weary of waiting. First I watched some soldiers drilling while an officer hollered at them. This made me uncomfortably aware of how soon they might be marching towards an enemy. The sun became very hot and I pulled up my bonnet and tightened its strings.

That was when I saw the boy. He was squatting a few feet away, playing with a whirligig.

Of course boys do not interest me in the least, but this one looked lonely. He was well-dressed, but his face was sad. He was not enjoying himself, just listlessly watching his toy.

"May I try it?" I asked. He jumped like a startled animal, although I am sure he must have noticed me watching him.

He shrugged, but came closer and sat down beside me, keeping his head down. He handed me the whirligig and watched me attach the string to each hand and whirl the disk. It was made out of a pewter button. I have often played with whirligigs at school and was proud of how fast I could make the button spin when I stretched out the string.

I asked the boy if he lived in the fort, but he told me he resides in town. His English accent intrigued me. Then he said something very surprising. He lives in Government House with General Brock! The boy's parents were both drowned. Brock was a friend of his father and is bringing up Ellis — that is the boy's name.

Of course I asked him to tell me about the famous general. Ellis said he is a great gentleman, but that he does not see him very often. Ellis was looking forward to his arrival this afternoon.

"I am proud to be his ward," Ellis told me. He is looked after by Porter, Brock's servant. That is why he was at the fort today. Usually he attends Mr. Cockerell's school in town, but today being a holiday he accompanied Porter to the fort to deliver some papers.

Ellis told me he is ten (although he is taller than I). He is very polite, much more so than any other boy I have met. His skin is pale and his hair as red as a rooster's. He had a strange look in his eyes, as if he were haunted by something. I imagine he misses his parents very much.

He offered to show me around the fort. I hesitated a second, then disobeyed Papa and followed Ellis.

The fort is vast inside, with many buildings. We peeked into the soldiers' barracks and I was surprised to see women and children in there. Ellis told me that some soldiers bring their families with them and this was their living quarters. One woman gestured for us to come in, but it looked so crowded and dark that I shook my head.

Then we scrambled up the massive earthen ramparts that surround the fort. On them are cannons on scrubbed wooden decks pointing out over the river. We squeezed in front of one of the cannons to see the view. The Niagara River flowed beneath us — there is a lighthouse at its mouth. Fort Niagara is directly across from Fort George.

I have never before realized how close the United States is. If there is a war, the enemy will be less than a mile away! I touched the cold metal of the cannon that is poised to fire across the river. My heart pounded so strongly I was sure Ellis could hear it.

He took me to the Cavalier Bastion, a large battery that General Brock is having constructed.

Many soldiers were working on it. "If we are attacked, this will overwhelm Fort Niagara," Ellis said proudly. That made my heart pound even harder. He showed me the bombproof dugouts — he called them "casemates" — in the earthen walls.

A soldier told us we were in the way so we went back to the bench. I was relieved that Papa had not returned to find me gone.

Ellis did not like to meet my eyes, but stared at the ground as I told him about the farm and school and Abbie. We were having such a good conversation — even though I was doing most of the talking — that I did not even notice Papa until he was standing over me.

Ellis jumped up and bowed to Papa, then scurried away like a scared rabbit. I told Papa that he lived with General Brock.

"I have heard of that boy," said Papa. "It is very considerate of Brock to give him a home. The General must be kind as well as important."

Papa and I went back to town for dinner. Then Mama, Maria, Hannah and I watched the muster of troops on the plain. What a sight it was! Since Papa has just been made Major Commandant of the Niagara Light Dragoons, he marched at the head of his new unit. Hamilton is a lieutenant and was close behind, as was James.

Maria found Charles and glued her eyes to him. I was proud of how handsome the men looked in their new uniforms of blue coats and curved swords.

The British troops were also a splendid sight, their scarlet coats and their swords and badges glittering in the sun. The soldiers' steps perfectly matched the rhythm of the fife and drums, as they marched with their odd stiff-legged stride. As they passed a tall soldier they saluted him — Mama said it was General Brock! I squinted to see him but he was so far away that he was a blur of red.

The stirring music made me want to march, myself. Several barking dogs followed the band and one who looked like Jack nipped at their feet!

We laughed at the Sedentary Militia, dressed in their own clothes and shuffling along out of step. Some carried hoes, canes or sticks instead of muskets! I spotted Mr. Seabrook, scowling heavily.

Somehow, watching the parade quelled the fear I had felt in the fort. It was such a grand spectacle that it seemed like a story or a game, something fashioned sheerly for our pleasure instead of for war.

At the end there was a gun salute to the King. What a commotion! First a cannon boomed, then muskets began firing in rapid succession from one end of the line to the other. Then all the soldiers fired their muskets at once. The field was filled with such a thick cloud of white smoke that the soldiers were obscured. The gunpowder smelled like rotten eggs.

Tabitha would have liked to hear this salute. She is very fond of the King, who is ill. His son, the Regent, rules in his stead.

Tonight is going to seem dreary compared with the rest of the day and I probably will not write any more. Everyone else is going to the ball and I have to stay here with sour Hannah.

Later

It is very late now, but I must tell you some more. The evening was not dreary after all! First I said goodbye to my family. I was proud of how elegant they looked. Papa and Hamilton were very tidy in their dark blue coats, stockings and breeches. I had polished their shoe buckles until they sparkled. Mama wore her best black lace gown and had a tall feather in her hair. She is such a handsome woman for her age.

Maria was dazzling. I had helped her take her short front hair out of its papers and it curled pleasingly on her forehead. The rest of her hair was drawn up on top and wound with intricate braids. Her new dress hung perfectly. She looked much older than fifteen, but she kissed me good-bye with great nervousness, asking me to pray that Charles would ask her to dance. I will not pray for something so frivolous, but I do hope she enjoys herself.

Hannah grumbled at me to stay out of her way, but when I asked her if I could go outside she refused to allow it. So I sat at the window watching all the ladies and gentlemen walk or ride to the ball. It was very light out and I felt sorry for myself that I was trapped inside.

Then I saw Ellis! He was sitting on the steps of Government House, looking as forlorn as I. I called to him and he sprang up and came to my window. He asked me to come down. I hesitated, then told him to meet me at the side of his house.

I crept down the stairs and peeked in the kitchen. Hannah had her back to me, washing dishes. Quickly and silently I crept across the hall, let myself out, and ran to the side of Government House. Ellis smiled for the first time when he saw me. He looks much less haunt-ed when he smiles.

What a fine time we had! There were so many people on the streets that nobody noticed us join-ing them on the way to the ball. Many of the ladies and gentlemen were even more resplendently dressed than my family. I could not stop staring.

We did not dare go into the dancing, of course, but we peeked in the doors and windows. A regimental band was playing and about fifty couples danced while others watched. I looked for all the members of my family, pointing them out to Ellis. Hamilton and Catherine danced the Allemande, as did Mama and Papa. How blissful Hamilton looked! I could not spot Maria for a long time. Then I was relieved to discover her in the Cotillion opposite Charles.

Ellis showed me the tall figure of General Brock, in the centre of a group of ladies, but all I could see was the back of his head and then he moved to another room. "I brought him a glass of ale before he came," Ellis told me proudly. "He was greatly looking forward to the dancing."

We finally grew tired of watching, and walked back. Now it was dark, but many houses glowed with light — what an enormous number of candles they must have! Laughter and music drifted out of their open windows. A group of men staggered by, singing drunkenly. It was so bright and lively compared to the country — the air seemed to hum with excitement.

Ellis invited me inside his house. It is grand but stark. He showed me General Brock's study, tiptoeing around it as if it were a shrine. What a great number of books lined the walls! The general's aides, Captain Glegg and Lieutenant Colonel Macdonell, also live in the house. Ellis often helps Porter serve them meals or shine their boots.

We went up to Ellis's room, a little one in the attic, and he taught me some of the fundamentals of chess. He has a set carved out of ivory that belonged to his father. I liked the game very much and he said I was a fast learner.

Ellis told me a little about his former life. He was born in England but came to Upper Canada with his parents when he was four. His father, Captain Babcock, was stationed in York. For most of his life Ellis lived in barracks, accompanying his parents wherever they were sent. He did not speak about their accident and I could tell he did not wish to.

He began to tell me more about General Brock — how he liked to read Homer and had lent the *Odyssey* and the *Iliad* to Ellis. "The General's favourite character is Ulysses, but I think he is more like Achilles," said Ellis, a strange look in his eyes. "In fact, he is too much like him."

Mama has read Homer, but she says he is too difficult for me. Ellis seems very advanced for his age. I did not understand what he was saying about General Brock and Achilles, or why he looked so anxious as he was speaking, but I am flattered at how much he talked to me.

I have now changed my mind about boys — not all are as disagreeable as Elias.

I left when we both grew so drowsy that we could not concentrate on chess. I was worried that Hannah would catch me, but I sneaked in with no trouble. She had fallen asleep in front of the kitchen fire. I went to bed and barely noticed Maria creeping in beside me several hours later.

5 June 1812

Dear Constance,

All morning Maria has been chattering to me about the ball, about the magnificent dresses and the dashing officers, and the huge supper of pigeons, duck, crawfish, tortoises, puddings and cheeses. She danced with Charles three times — of course I could not tell her I had watched! She would not approve of my being so bold, and I smiled to myself with my secret.

I am too weary to write much about the rest of today. I had to put on my best gown and slippers and accompany Mama and Maria on several calls. It was tiresome to sit still with nothing to do but listen to the ladies' gossip. Hamilton went to the horse racing and I wish I could have gone with him. All day I wondered what Ellis was doing, but although I looked for him out of the window several times, I did not see him.

The weather being so fine, tomorrow we are driving to the Falls! I will finally see them and am eagerly anticipating the journey.

6 June 1812

Dear Constance,

Maria is already asleep, but today's excursion was so delightful that I must tell you all about it before I join her.

We left at dawn, except for Hamilton. He and Charles were attending the horse racing again. Maria wanted to go with them but Mama said it would not be suitable.

The road first went along the bank of the river. It was very picturesque, bordered by orchards and fields. Queenston is at the base of the Heights. It is a fine place with a harbour full of boats and the banks of the river rising steeply on either side — no wonder they are called the Heights! Papa was very interested to see two ships, the *Royal George* and the *Gloster*, anchored at the wharf. "They must have brought us more recruits," he said. He sounded pleased and I tried not to think about why. Many other boats were unloading supplies. About twenty buildings were scattered among the orchards and gardens. The river was so narrow — Papa said barely two hundred yards! I shivered inside as I pointed out to Maria the closeness of the United States. This did not seem to worry her as it does me.

Mama then reminded us how she, Papa, Caroline and Hamilton had disembarked at Queenston when they first came to Upper Canada. Is it truly possible that we will have to fight against their former homeland? All these unsettling thoughts were spoiling my pleasure in the day, so I made a great effort to banish them.

We did not stop for dinner but had a picnic in the wagon as we ascended the steep Portage Road from the landing. It was amusing trying to balance our bread and cheese as the wagon jostled. Mama handed Papa bits of food while he drove, making us all laugh.

The scenery became more and more dramatic as we approached the Falls. We could hear their thunder long before we reached them.

What a sublime sight! The immense rush of water roared down and I pulled back my bonnet so I could feel the cold spray on my face. There are really three falls, the Horseshoe and Montmorency on our side and those of Fort Schlosser on the American side. On Table Rock, below, eagles were circling and screaming. Papa said rattlesnakes dwelt there.

Mama and Papa have seen the Falls several times but it was the first experience of them for Maria and me. We strolled and gazed in awe for almost an hour and could scarcely tear ourselves away. Mama said the Falls were an example of God's infinite power. As I watched them I felt soothed by their immense strength, as if God were taking care of the world and I only had to trust in His wisdom.

We finally had to leave because we had been invited for supper to the Hamiltons' in Queenston. Maria wanted first to call on the Secords, who also live there — Mrs. Secord is Charles's older sister. Mama scolded her, saying she does not yet know Charles well enough to visit his relatives. She reminded Maria that she is only fifteen. Maria sulked until the splendour of the Hamiltons' house distracted her.

I have never seen such a fine residence! It is a tall stone mansion on a cliff high above the river, with side wings and a covered gallery and four chimneys. Inside there is much elegant furniture.

The Hamiltons were very gracious. We were taken to wash off the grime of our journey, and then they gave us a bountiful supper. After the meal Mrs. Hamilton begged Mama to entertain us on the pianoforte. Because the Hamiltons are Scottish, she honoured them by playing a reel.

I cannot write about the journey back to Niagara, as I slept all the way. But I revived when we reached the town. A light was burning in Ellis's window. I wonder if he has ever been to the Falls?

7 June 1812

Dear Constance,

We are home now. Maria and I have just had a long discussion about which we prefer, the town or the farm. Maria says she wishes we lived in Niagara all the time. Of course, all she wants to do is attend more balls. I feel safer on the farm and I was very glad to see Tabitha and Jack again. In town I would not be permitted to go about alone as I do here, and I would have to spend too much time making dreary calls with Mama. I did find the bustle of people and activity exciting, however. Our tranquil life here now seems rather dull compared with Niagara.

I especially miss Ellis and wonder what he is doing and if I will ever see him again. What a pleasing boy he was! Elias and the others at school seem oafs compared to him. "Ellis" and

"Elias" are such similar names, and yet the two boys are so different.

Tonight as I sat on Papa's knee he told me that when he was younger he wore his hair in a queue! I teased him for having a pigtail hanging down his back. I enjoyed seeing so much of Papa in town. I wish he did not have to go back there as usual tomorrow.

8 June 1812

Dear Constance,

Everyone around me is lovesick again. At least Abbie is keeping her promise and does not speak about Uriah to me. But I have noticed how observant she is of his every move. I have not told her about Ellis. I fear she will conclude that I think of him the same way she thinks of Uriah, and that is not true.

Hamilton has once again asked Catherine to marry him and, once again, she says she is not ready to decide. He told me this as I rode with him to bring in the cows. "I will not give up," he said. He had tears in his eyes and I grieved for him. Catherine is always kind to me and I would very much like to have her as a sister.

Samuel called on Tabitha after supper and they sat in the kitchen for a long time. As for

Maria, I have told her I will not listen to her talk about the ball any longer. My ears will fall off if I hear any more!

9 June 1812

Dear Constance,

As I was helping Tabitha churn, she told me that Samuel has asked her to marry him! But, to my relief, she says she is not sure she wants to. He has a small house and makes little money as a hired hand. She does not think he is very bright. "I could do better," she sniffed.

Her decision seems so calculated. I wanted to ask her if she was in *love* with Samuel, as Hamilton certainly is with Catherine, but children are not supposed to speak of such things. So I have to talk to you about them instead.

10 June 1812

Dear Constance,

The weather is hot and the schoolroom is stuffy. At home everyone is irritable. Tabitha scolded me for letting Jack lick the meat platter. I do this every day and she has never objected before. We wash it well afterwards, so what harm can it do?

Mama scolded Maria for being indolent. Ever

since we returned she has not been sewing or reading or practising her singing or doing anything at all to improve herself. Maria wept all evening, in an irksome, self-indulgent manner that wore us all out.

Worst of all, the adults mutter to each other about war. I try to close my ears to their worried voices.

11 June 1812

Dear Constance,

Maria is acting very strangely. She spent all day in bed with a stomachache, which she says is caused by an ailment that I will begin to get every month when I am her age. I do not believe that — she is just making it up to annoy me.

She will not let me in the bedroom when she is dressing. Mama hovers around her and they whisper to each other. I would very much like to know their secret, but they will not tell me.

12 June 1812

Dear Constance,

Today was very frightening. It was the last day of school and unlike any other school day I have known.

We spent all morning having a spelling bee. I

won with the word "euchymous," beating even Conrad, who is the best speller in the school. (I do not know what that word means and it was a desperate guess.)

After dinner Mr. Simmons said we would do no more work for the day. Instead, anyone who wanted was allowed to choose a song to sing. Little Sarah chose "Baa, Baa Black Sheep." Elias led us in a rousing rendition of "The British Grenadiers." Then Nathaniel tried to teach us a song he learnt from his father called "The Cuckoo's Nest," but Mr. Simmons was very shocked and threatened to whip him if he did not stop.

I sang Tabitha's Napoleon lullaby alone, for no one else knew it. Everyone laughed. I have never sung in school before and, despite how my voice squeaked, it was a pleasant novelty.

Then came the frightening part. Mr. Simmons asked us each to say where we were from — that is, before we came to Upper Canada. Elizabeth and Elias and I are the only ones who were born here, whose families were Loyalists. Patrick and Robert are from Ireland, Ralph from England, Conrad from Germany and Henrik from Holland. But most of the class, like Abbie, are Americans.

"I want you to think about this," Mr. Simmons said quietly. "Almost all of you were born in the

United States or have families who were. Yet Britain may soon be asking you to fight your former homeland."

His words were like cold water, dispelling the warmth of the singing. Elias asked him what he meant.

Mr. Simmons said he meant, if there was a war — and he thought there *would* be one. I started to shiver inside. He told us how he had come to Upper Canada two years ago from Vermont, hoping to make a living here. But now he is returning!

He cannot stay in our country because the government is asking him to take an oath of allegiance to the King.

His voice became angry. He said, "He is not my king, and I fail to see how he is yours either — except for Robert, Ralph and Patrick. I am not going to find myself in the position of fighting my own countrymen." He is returning to Vermont tomorrow.

Nathaniel asked him who would be our teacher. Mr. Simmons said another teacher would be found. Then he dismissed school early. He said it was a pleasure instructing us and wished us luck in our future endeavours. He asked each of us to come up and shake his hand.

When it was my turn Mr. Simmons said I was

a very intelligent child and he hoped I would find a school that fulfilled my potential. I curtseyed and thanked him, but I was too frightened by what he had told us to be pleased by his compliment.

I am also feeling downcast because I will never again attend that school. Oh, Constance, why do things have to change?

13 June 1812

Dear Constance,

This morning in the barn I told Hamilton what Mr. Simmons had said. Hamilton said he was wise to leave now if he did not want to be involved. His voice was grave.

I could not stop myself from asking what I do not want to know — if there is going to be a war.

"There might be," said Hamilton. "I fervently hope not, but all signs are pointing to one."

I tried not to show him how terrifying I found his words. "If there is," I asked, my voice choking, "will we have to fight our former homeland, as Mr. Simmons said?"

"We are Upper Canadians now, not Americans. We are under British rule. If there is a war, we will have to fight for our king, just as Papa did during the Revolutionary War."

Now I could not keep back my tears. "Will Papa have to fight again? And you?"

Hamilton wiped my eyes with his handkerchief. "We will not have a choice, Susanna," he sighed. "Nobody I know wants a war, but we are trapped — caught between the Lion and the Eagle. I cannot see any way out, but I want you to be brave and not think about it."

I do not feel at all brave and I cannot stop thinking about it, Constance. You are the only person I can tell.

14 June 1812

Dear Constance,

There were not many in church this morning because there was only a lay preacher. Also, there were so many flies it was hard to pay attention. But Mr. Hartsell said something that comforted me — that God holds us in the palm of His hand.

All afternoon we stayed inside the hot house to escape the flies. I am covered in red welts from their bites. I began *Robinson Crusoe* for the third time and it was another solace to be immersed in the world of Crusoe's island. Mama usually does not let me read novels on Sundays but today she allowed it. Indeed, we were all immersed in books, a welcome relief from the flies.

Dear Constance,

Helping with the work at home is a welcome distraction from my fears. There is so much for me to do that I feel guilty that I escaped so many chores when I was in school.

Maria added to my guilt. She is recovered from her strange ailment, but still irritable. Because it is Monday, we spent the whole day doing laundry. I had forgotten how laborious it is, although it is much easier with the wash-house Hamilton built last year than it was doing it in the kitchen.

Tabitha scrubbed Hamilton's work clothes while Maria boiled the cottons, stirring them with a stick. The fire made the hot day even warmer and perspiration dripped in our eyes. I helped Mama pour boiling water over the finer linens. She let me swish the indigo bag through the water to blue them — I enjoy how it makes swirls of colour in the water. We dipped the coarse muslin into cold starch. Then we hung all the larger articles on the clothesline.

As I was helping Maria hang the clothes I made the mistake of complaining that we had not yet had dinner. She replied, scowling, that when I was in school they often missed dinner completely on Mondays, and that I was lucky not to have to do laundry for most of the year.

She is right, of course, but she injured my feelings by saying so. I was glad to leave her and help Mama spread the smaller articles on the grass. I sprinkled them with a watering can so they would bleach more thoroughly, enjoying this so much that the sting of Maria's words diminished. And when we were finally finished, and had eaten our very late meal, Mama allowed me to be free for the rest of the afternoon.

I did not go to Abbie's, because they would be doing laundry also. But I had an enjoyable time trying to persuade Sukie to jump over a log. She would not, the stubborn animal, so I got off and enticed Jack, who had come with us, to do it. We both leapt back and forth, Jack barking with joy. Sometimes he seems more like a person than a dog — his lip curls up as if he is trying to smile.

A breeze kept away most of the flies, the air smelt sweet and I found some early strawberries. Most pleasant of all is not to have to sit in the dark schoolhouse making endless lists!

16 June 1812

Dear Constance,

This morning we did the ironing — or, rather, Mama and Maria and Tabitha did. It is so diffi-

cult to get the iron heated to the right tempera-
ture, and to curl the ruffles on Papa's and Hamilton's shirts, that I am not yet entrusted with
this task. Mine is to hang the pressed clothes all
over the house to air. How fresh everything
smelled!

After dinner I had to do my needlework — I
am sewing handkerchiefs. Finally I was permit
ted to ride over to Abbie's, where I spent the rest
of the afternoon helping her take care of Paul and
Johnny. They are such lively imps and it was difficult to keep them out of mischief. But we took
them to the creek, where they were so absorbed
in paddling and digging in the mud that Abbie
and I could finally talk.We waved branches to
keep away the flies, but one flew into my mouth
and I spat it out with disgust.

"Do you think there will be a war?" she asked
me.

This is the first time we have talked about it.
All I could answer was that I hoped not. We
dared to voice our fears to each other — would
there be fighting right around us? Would we be
safe? And, worst of all, would the men in our families be killed? It was terrifying, but also a relief,
to say these dreadful things out loud.

Abbie is worried about her father. He talks

all the time about how he is American-born and does not believe in fighting for Britain — just like Mr. Simmons. Besides, he has not time for it, what with making their new home. That is what he came to Upper Canada for, not to fight.

I asked her if he had taken the oath to the King that Mr. Simmons talked about. Abbie looked scared. She said he did, when they first came here, but only so he could get land. He is going to ignore it.

How Papa would disapprove of this if he knew of it! Abbie clutched my arm. "Susanna, what will happen to my father? I do not want him to fight, but will he be arrested if he refuses? Or will we have to go back to the United States like Mr. Simmons?"

These questions were so confusing that I could not answer. We looked at each other with despair. Finally I told her what Hamilton suggested, to try not to think about it.

So we jumped up and decided to swim. We took off our shoes and stockings and dresses and petticoats and pantalets and, wearing just our shifts, went into the creek. The little boys, who cannot swim, cheered us on from the shore.

Hamilton has taught me how to swim but I am so skinny I have to really struggle to stay afloat.

Abbie, being chubbier, is much more proficient. We splashed and dived and blew out water from our mouths. Then we undressed the boys, each took one, and walked with him into the deeper water.

How they squealed and shrieked! I had Johnny and it was like trying to hold on to a wriggling, slippery fish. I swished him back and forth in the water while he crowed with joy.

Finally we all sat in the hot sun until we were dry enough to put on our clothes. Johnny burrowed into my lap and then fell asleep as I held him. Abbie is so lucky to have little brothers, even though she does not think so.

Tonight Maria scolded me about my dirty feet and made me wash them thoroughly before I sat down to write in here. She is still in a disagreeable mood and I am weary of it.

These are such peaceful days. I cannot bear that anything will happen to disturb them. *Do not think about it.*

17 June 1812

Dear Constance,

Tonight Maria forgot to tighten the ropes on the bed, and when she got in she collapsed onto the floor! You should have seen her with her legs up and the rest of her sunk in the mattress! I could not stop laughing. After a minute she started laughing too, and now we are friends again.

18 June 1812

Dear Constance,

Hamilton is wretched. Catherine and her parents have moved back to New York in case there is a war.

Before she left she promised him her hand. Because Catherine's father thinks Hamilton is too young, however, they have to wait two years to be betrothed. Thus her promise is a secret, which I am not to tell anyone.

Hamilton's joy at Catherine's acceptance is cancelled by his misery at her leaving. I have never seen him so dejected. Tabitha made him his favourite pudding for supper to cheer him up, but it did not help. He would not join us in the parlour but sat on the porch drawing on his pipe, an anguished expression on his face that I have never seen before. I tried to comfort him but he told me he wanted to be alone.

It seems inconceivable that Catherine and her family will be living in a country that could be our enemy. Oh, Constance, I am trying to be brave, but tonight it is impossible.

19 June 1812

Dear Constance,

I am going to try to simply tell you what I do each day instead of agonizing about what could happen. We spent the morning weeding and the afternoon quilting. I enjoy choosing each piece of fabric. One square of pink dimity is from a dress I had when I was five! I remember how proud of it I was.

In the afternoon the shoemaker came by. He has not been in this district for months and there were several pairs of Hamilton's and Papa's boots for him to patch. Tomorrow Caroline and James are arriving to visit us. It will be a great pleasure to see Caroline again.

20 June 1812

Dear Constance,

Do you have a sister, I wonder? Mine is very difficult. I am not talking about Maria. Despite how much she sometimes aggravates me we are fond of each other. I am speaking of Caroline.

When Caroline lived with us she was serious but kind. She showed me how to knit and was always interested in my doings. Now all she does is criticize.

Caroline is very religious, but in a different

71

way from Mama and Hamilton. They have both taught me that God is loving. Caroline thinks He is revengeful, exacting punishment on those who do not do His will. I much prefer Mama and Hamilton's God to hers.

My troubles began as soon as Caroline and James arrived this evening. As we sat in the parlour I could not stop staring at Caroline's bulging front. The last time I saw her she was not showing at all. What a miracle it is that God has placed a child inside her!

But when I expressed my wonder at how large she was growing she said she was shocked, and that little girls should not say such things.

Papa, who had come home a day early to see Caroline, told her not to be so harsh. He gestured for me to come and sit on his lap, which I was glad to do.

Caroline answered that I should be reprimanded. When nobody did so, she frowned at me. I frowned back. Why has she changed so much?

21 June 1812

Dear Constance,

It is not Christian to hate one's sister. But tonight I have to confess to you that I do. I will tell you the whole sad story.

This morning there were many people in church because Reverend Addison from Niagara was there. I thought he preached an excellent sermon, about how we should trust in the goodness of God as a tree planted by water spreads its roots and draws up nourishment. My icy fears melted at his words and I felt more hopeful than I have for a long time.

We sang two of my favourite hymns — "Lo! He Comes with Clouds Descending" and "What Wondrous Love Is This." Maria was standing next to me and I let my croaky voice blend into her pure one. Abbie was sitting behind us and we smiled at each other often.

Papa and Hamilton, who greatly admire Reverend Addison, talked to him after the service while Abbie and I chased Paul and Johnny all around the churchyard. When I got into the wagon I felt utterly content with the morning.

But Caroline shattered my bliss. On the drive home she could do nothing but criticize. She thought the sermon was weak and the singing too boisterous. Hamilton, who is still wretched from Catherine's departure, disagreed with her. They argued so violently that Papa had to tell them to be quiet.

When we got home Caroline took me aside and told me it was not respectful to run around the churchyard, and that I should not have kept looking at Abbie during the service. She accused me of not paying proper attention. When I retorted that I could repeat the whole sermon she ignored me.

At dinner she said my table manners were appalling, just because I took a piece of pork that Hamilton did not want, from his plate. She said I did not sit straight enough in my chair. After we ate she inspected my workbox and said it was untidy. Then she asked to see my sampler and criticized how little work I had done on it since the last time she was here.

Mama told her she was not being fair, that I have too much other needlework to have time for my sampler — especially since I do not get much sewing done when I am at school.

"I do not approve of Susanna going to school," said Caroline. "Girls should stay home and help their mothers."

I could tell that Mama was trying to keep her temper, as she changed the subject and asked Caroline what she had made for the baby. My face burned as I bent over my sampler. No, I have not spent much time on it, but what I have done is good work, neat and clean. I have finished the numbers and am halfway through the alphabet. Then all I have to do is choose a proverb for the top. Mama says I am as accomplished a sewer as she is herself.

When I had stitched the N I asked Mama if I could read. She nodded and I took down *Robinson Crusoe*.

"What is that, Susanna?" Caroline asked sharply.

I showed her.

She said it was not at all suitable for Sundays and asked where the book was that she had given me for my last birthday.

Sighing, I put away my beloved *Crusoe* and took down *A Token for Children* instead. It is a hateful book, all about children who go to Hell because they are sinful. All about Caroline's God.

The day got much worse. I was so angry at Caroline that I was, I admit, deliberately naughty. I am ashamed to tell you what I did, but I must if I am to be honest.

The stern, smug expression on her face every time Caroline looked at me, so different from her former kindness, impelled me to do it. While she was teaching Maria a new stitch, I crept out of the room and found Caroline's new parasol. It is a very handsome one, with a handle shaped like a bird and much lace and ribbons.

I took it into the kitchen — luckily Tabitha was in her room. We had no molasses but I carefully smeared honey onto each of its spokes. Then I closed it up again.

I assumed that Caroline would not notice what I had done until she opened her parasol the next day, too far away to scold me. But when they were leaving she picked up the parasol and the honey started dripping down. She then made the mistake of opening it further. Despite my dismay, her shriek was very satisfying.

Of course I had to admit my crime. Hamilton laughed and laughed, and Papa looked as if he wanted to. Maria, who had also been impatient with Caroline, stared at me with shocked admiration.

I thought Caroline would split with anger. "She should be whipped!" she gasped, wiping honey from her hair. "I have never known a child so spoilt! Mine will not be allowed to get away with such behaviour."

Mama ordered me to go to my bedroom immediately, in a quiet voice which shattered me.

I lay on the bed, bitterly regretting what I had done. *Would* Mama whip me? I knew I deserved it, but she never had.

I am too ashamed to tell you what Mama said when she came up. She did not whip me but talked long and seriously about how wrong I was. Then I knelt at her feet and asked God to forgive me.

Mama kissed me and told me she hoped that tomorrow I would be the good daughter I usually was.

I hope I will be too. But I am still angry at Caroline, for if she had not been so cruel to me I would never have acted as I did today.

22 June 1812

Dear Constance,

I helped Tabitha all day with the cooking to prove to Mama that I was good again. Tabitha is a plain cook. She usually scoffs at the recipes in the cookbook Papa bought Mama last year. To-day, however, I persuaded her to try an unusual one for syllabub, without any sugar or eggs. First we put some beer and cider into a punch bowl and grated in nutmeg. Then I took the bowl to the barn and asked Ben to milk the cow into it. We let it stand for an hour, then scattered currants over the top. I sat in suspense at the supper table until it was time to taste it, but we all found it delicious. Mama praised me for encouraging Tabitha to be adventurous.

23 June 1812

Dear Constance,

I am trying to write calmly, but it is difficult. I do not like growing older. When I was little I would fall asleep on my stool by the fire when Mama and Papa talked about their past, or I would only hear part of the story. Now I am wide awake and what I hear is increasingly disturbing.

Papa had come home for the day, to share with us a letter he received from New Brunswick. It is the first time he has heard from his father for over a year. The letter said that the New Brunswick family is thriving and well.

Our grandmother died several years ago. Hamilton has met our grandfather, but I probably never will. The letter prompted Papa and Mama to talk affectionately about the relatives they have not seen for so long.

But then their talk became bitter. Papa began speaking of his brothers, especially Shubal. He related again how Shubal had been shot by Rebels. "If there is a war I will not be sorry to fight that country," he said.

Mama was very upset. "Thomas, remember that I still have family in the United States!" she told him.

"Remember also that Richard was killed by

the same Rebels who killed Shubal," Papa replied.

"How can you speak so? Those days are over! We have to forget about killing and revenge! I never want to live through times like that again!" She began to weep.

Papa patted her arm, but he made her weep harder when he said quietly, "I am sorry, Polly, but we may *have* to."

No one noticed me slip out of the room and come up here to write to you. I cannot *bear* to hear them talk about war — not the previous one and especially not the one that might happen. It also shocks me greatly to hear Mama and Papa disagree. They have never done so before.

I am going to blow out the candle and go to bed.

24 June 1812

Dear Constance,

I am broken-hearted. A skunk has broken into the henhouse and eaten my favourite hen, the little white one I called Snowflake. She always came running up first when I went out with the food. But this morning only her head and claws were left. I knew it was a skunk because of the dreadful odour. Hamilton patched up the hole where it got in and tried to comfort me, but I cannot help weeping. How can such an exquisite creature be alive one day and dead the next?

25 June 1812

Dear Constance,

It was very hot today and Mama, Maria and I took a picnic to the creek. They paddled and I swam. Maria would not come in past her ankles — she says swimming is not ladylike. She used to enjoy it as much as I. What airs she puts on! I hope she will not change as much as Caroline has.

Mama dried my wet hair and I leaned against her. For the first time in many days I felt at peace.

26 June 1812

Dear Constance,

It is still extremely hot. The air is heavy and moist, like a weight pressing on us. Mrs. Seabrook finds it very trying due to her condition, and has taken to her bed. Abbie has to do all the cooking and thus I scarcely see her.

Dear Constance,

A storm has relieved us of the oppressive weather. Thunder sounded closer and closer and the rain gushed down in the afternoon. I was so glad to see it that I ran outside and danced in the yard, holding my face up to the coolness. Tabitha pulled me inside in case I got struck by lightning. I went upstairs to put on dry clothes and laughed at Maria cowering under the covers. She has always been frightened of thunder, whereas I find it exhilarating.

The storm diminished to a light rain. Mama and Hamilton went to call on the Paulings, and Maria, Tabitha and I sat in front of the kitchen fire. Tabitha told us some of the ghostly stories from her homeland, about bogles and boggarts and witches and black dogs. The scary tales made us draw closer to each other, but each time she finished one we begged for another.

The last one she told was about the moon being buried in a marsh. Tabitha has a low, compelling voice and I could see the white faces and empty eye sockets of the dead people who rose out of the water. It brought back the fear that lurks so close to me these days. The story has a happy ending, for the forces of good win over the forces of evil. But I could not shake off my dread. *Please*, God, do not let it happen.

28 June 1812

Dear Constance,

God did not hear me, for it has happened. We are at war. I am so frightened I can hardly hold this pen, but perhaps if I tell you about everything my heart will stop hurting so much.

We were all asleep when there was a loud pounding at the door. Outside, Jack barked frantically. Maria and I both sat up at the same time. We heard Hamilton go down the stairs.

I went to the window and opened it. At the door was our neighbour, Mr. Culp. Hamilton let him in and I could not hear what they were saying. About half an hour later Mr. Culp galloped off. I wanted to go down and ask Hamilton what it was about, but Maria would not let me.

When he told us this morning Mama started weeping. "Not another war!" she kept saying. "Oh, my poor boy. What will happen to you and Thomas? I *cannot* bear it." She was so wretched that she went back to bed and stayed there for most of the day. I kept bringing her cups of tea and bits of food to tempt her, but she would not eat.

I could not comfort her. Indeed, she scarcely seemed to notice me, but seemed far away, weeping softly and whispering Richard's name. To see her like this frightened me even more than the news of war.

Hamilton told Maria and Tabitha and I everything Mr. Culp had said. Apparently the officers at Fort George were entertaining the officers of Fort Niagara when they got word that their two countries were at war. The American officers stayed to finish dinner, then went back across the river. How very strange, to be one minute friends and the next, enemies.

Although today is Sunday, Papa has not come home. I wonder if he was at the dinner? General Brock is arriving at Fort George from York today.

I asked Hamilton what he would do. He said he did not know, but he soon found out. A few hours later a rider came with a message from Papa. Hamilton was to assemble the men in the vicinity and to march them down to Fort George as soon as possible. He put on his uniform and immediately rode to the inn, where the companies were gathering.

Then I had to comfort both Maria and Tabitha, for Charles and Samuel would be fighting also. We did not have much time for weeping, however, for we had to quickly pack Hamilton's box with flannel shirts, blankets and medicine. I slipped in some of his favourite comforts.

We only saw Hamilton again briefly, when he returned to say goodbye. He went upstairs to Mama first. When he came down he could scarcely contain his words as he described all the men who were waiting for him to lead them to Fort George.

I asked him if Mr. Seabrook was there. "Yes, he was," said Hamilton, "although I have never seen a fellow who looked less eager to fight. Many of the men share his reluctance. It is going to be difficult to rouse their enthusiasm."

Hamilton's own enthusiasm, so different from the dejection he has felt since Catherine left, disturbed me greatly. I reminded him how he had not wanted a war.

"I do *not* want a war," he answered. "But if we have to have one, I am glad to do my duty. And it is something new — anything new is pleasing."

My brother is very different from me.

Hamilton kissed Maria, then me. He instructed me to be brave, to help Mama, and to pray for him and Papa. "Write in your journal every day," he advised me. "It will help you to stay steady." I forced back my tears as I promised him I would do so.

Tabitha was angrily clattering pots in the corner. Hamilton shook her hand and said he would take good care of Samuel, who is in Hamilton's unit.

As he galloped off my tears erupted. "How can Hamilton be so willing to go to war? He could be killed!" I collapsed into a chair.

Maria put her arms around me, wiping her own eyes. She said men thought differently from women. Tabitha agreed. "It is a game to them," she muttered. "The men fight and the women suffer." She began to weep as well, remembering her father and brother.

After a few minutes, however, she stood up. "Enough of this," she told us. "Crying will not help." She made us all some tea and I felt slightly calmer.

Then Maria and I went upstairs to comfort Mama. To my great relief she was out of bed and herself again. We knelt and prayed that the war would be short and that the men in our family, Papa and Hamilton and James, would be kept safe. I knew Maria was silently saying a prayer for Charles, and I added one for Samuel.

Mama said we would have to take care of the men's work as well as our own, since of course Ben, our hired hand, has gone to fight as well. Tabitha will do the milking and Maria will help more with the cooking. I will feed the pigs and take the cows out to pasture and back. Mama is worried about the harvest, but she said that perhaps the war will be over by then. Oh, please may that be true, Constance!

I am amazed by how quickly Mama has regained her strength. I wish I shared her courage. She says that all we can do is try to bear this. But I do not think I can. It is as if the dark creatures from Tabitha's stories were suddenly real.

Maria is crying softly in bed. When will I see Hamilton and Papa again? Will anything ever be the same?

29 June 1812

Dear Constance,

We were numb today, going about our chores silently and wondering what the men were doing. Are they already fighting? Will the enemy come here? If they do, how will we protect ourselves? We have only the rifle that hangs above the kitchen fire, and none of us knows how to use it.

30 June 1812

Dear Constance,

Last night I woke up screaming from the most dreadful nightmare I have ever had. Napoleon was in it, and wolves and boggarts and ghosts, and Uncle Richard lying in a field, and Uncle Shubal with a gaping wound, and poor mangled Snowflake. Maria stroked my hair and comforted me and I was glad to have someone to hold on to. Now it is after breakfast and I am still so shaky I do not know how I will get through the rest of the day.

1 July 1812

Dear Constance,

I am slightly less frightened, for nothing is happening and it is hard to believe there really *is* a war — except for the deep ache of missing Hamilton and Papa.

One of the cats has had six kittens. Their tiny mews as they nestle in the straw lighten my gloom. Hamilton would have drowned them, for we have too many cats, but with his absence they are reprieved and I can watch them grow.

2 July 1812
Late

Dear Constance,

The cherries are ripe and I ate so many I had to go out in the night to use the privy. The air was cool and sweet. I do not believe Maria when she says that night air is poison. I wish she would let me open the window — our room is so stuffy and hot.

An owl was calling and the stars shone like millions of distant candles. Their immensity soothes me the way the Falls did. Surely God, who made such marvels, will keep us safe.

3 July 1812

Dear Constance,

When the kittens sleep they are one furry lump. I have carefully picked them up and examined them. They look like mice with their closed eyes and tiny flat ears. I have named them Whiskers, Wiggle, Crusoe, George (after the King), Blackie and Mouse. Mouse is my favourite — she has soft grey fur just like a mouse. We have always called their mother simply the Striped Cat, but I have renamed her Patience, because she is such a patient mother. I have put them all in a box lined with straw, so that the other cats will not bother them. Jack has sniffed them curiously but does not harm them.

4 July 1812

Dear Constance,

It is increasingly difficult to believe we are at war. With the men gone it is very quiet. I am only allowed to leave the yard when I take out the cows, so I have not seen Abbie since war was declared. Mama is worried that we will be looted, as she was in South Carolina. But no one comes.

I will tell you what my days are now like. I get up and help Tabitha with the milking. At first my fingers were not strong enough to bring down the milk, but now I am becoming an expert. I enjoy the pinging sound as the warm milk gushes into the empty pail, but it is hard to carry the pail back to the house — Tabitha has to help me. Before I do I give some of the warm milk to Patience.

Then I take the cows out to pasture, riding Sukie. It is difficult to get them going in one direction — I have to use a long switch — but Jack helps me. The rest of the day I assist with the chores and the cooking. There is so much to do that the only time I have to see the kittens is when I take out the scraps to feed the pigs.

In the evenings we all sit in the parlour — Tabitha sits with us, which she never did when Hamilton and Papa were here. We sew or knit while Mama reads aloud. Right now we are listening to *Pilgrim's Progress*, which is completely engrossing. The evenings are so light I would like to be outside, but Mama does not allow it. Every night we end with a song or a hymn. Then

Mama leads us in prayer before we retire.

She says it is important to be cheerful and I am trying my best to be so. This is easier during the busy day than at night in bed, when all I can think about is Hamilton and Papa.

5 July 1812

Dear Constance,

We have heard from Papa! A dragoon from his regiment arrived with a letter. It was much too short. All Papa said was that he and Hamilton are safe and have not done any fighting so far. He sent us his love and said he will try to write every two weeks. He told us not to write back unless it was an emergency, since it would be difficult to locate him and Hamilton.

"Your father has never been one to write long letters," Mama said fondly. "At least we know they are safe. That is all that matters." Her voice was brave but she stroked the paper with a trembling hand.

The letter raises so many questions, I would almost rather not have received it at all. If Papa and Hamilton are difficult to locate, are they not at Fort George? If they are not fighting, what are they doing? Are they telling the truth about being safe, or are they just reassuring us?

I ran out to the barn to seek comfort from the

kittens. They still just sleep and eat. Crusoe is the most vigorous sucker and pushes the others out of his way. Patience patiently grooms each one in turn. I am eager for them to open their eyes and play.

I sat for an hour in the barn watching them. It is so warm and dark and peaceful there.

6 July 1812

Dear Constance,

Today Tabitha was telling me how much she missed Samuel. I reminded her that she said he was not very bright and that she could do better. She denied it hotly, stating Samuel is a fine and decent man and I should not insult him.

I suppose the war has made her realize she loves him after all. Does that mean she will leave us and get married when the war is over? I want it to end, of course, but I cannot bear the idea of losing Tabitha.

7 July 1812

Dear Constance,

The mosquitoes are so bad that I had to wear a veil over my face while picking cherries. I pitted a bowl full and Tabitha made a delicious cherry pie. We are lucky that we have enough food. There is plenty of salt pork and dried meat, we have eggs and milk, and our garden and orchard are bountiful.

I wonder how Abbie's family is faring with Mr. Seabrook gone? I asked Mama if I could take over some cherries to them, but she is afraid to let me go. They have a cow and a garden, so at least I know they are not hungry.

8 July 1812

Dear Constance,

The kittens' eyes are partly open and they stumble around in the straw, having mock fights with each other. Crusoe is still the strongest but Mouse is the largest female. I snuggle her to me until she cries for her mother.

I cannot help imagining what dreadful things might be happening to Hamilton and Papa.

9 July 1812

Dear Constance,

I hardly slept last night because of mosquitoes. Despite the closed window they seem to get into the room. Maria got cross because I tried to make a tent out of the sheet, leaving her exposed. But mosquitoes do not seem to bother her. I am miserable with itchy bites.

10 July 1812

Dear Constance,

Because we are only women now, we often talk about things that would be unsuitable if the men were here. Tonight Mama greatly surprised me by saying that, before she had Caroline, she lost two babies. Their names were Amy and Phoebe and both of them died at birth.

Amy and Phoebe . . . two little sisters whom I will never know.

After Phoebe was born, Mama almost died also. Giving birth can be dangerous, of course — last year one of our neighbours, Mr. Metler, lost his young wife and twin infants. Mama is very worried about Caroline, who is alone in Burlington. She would like to bring her here, but we have no safe way of doing that.

11 July 1812

Dear Constance,

Sometimes I grow weary of writing in here every night, for there is nothing of interest to tell — except that the kittens' eyes are now fully open. Sometimes I would like to give up this journal, but I will try to keep it up for Hamilton's sake.

Dear Constance,

There has been no church since the war began, so as usual Mama read the service to us. She does this better than Papa did, who spoke the words too quickly. But how I miss his voice! And Hamilton's strong one ringing out the responses! I am tired of seeing the same three faces every day, dear as they are to me. My world has shrunk so small that sometimes I feel I can scarcely breathe.

13 July 1812

Dear Constance,

Tabitha has always spoken freely to me and Maria, but since we sit together every evening she is now growing just as comfortable with Mama. Tonight she was telling us about a form of divination from the Bible that she used to do in England. After she described it, Maria begged Mama to let us try it. To my surprise, and Maria's, Mama agreed.

Tabitha got the large house key and placed it in the Bible, over the seventh verse of the last chapter of the Song of Solomon. She instructed Maria to take off her right garter and tie the Bible shut with it, with the bow of the key sticking out. Then she and Maria suspended the Bible in the air by balancing either side of the bow on their two middle fingers.

"We will start with Maria," said Tabitha. "A." Together they chanted part of the verse: "Many waters cannot quench love, neither can the floods drown it." Then Tabitha said "B" and they repeated the chant. At C the key turned! Tabitha caught the Bible before it fell to the floor.

"C!" cried Maria, with a shriek. "I will marry someone whose name begins with C!" She pranced around the room. I accused her of turning the key herself and she objected.

Then we tried Tabitha. I got very tired of hearing them repeat the verse again and again. At S, however, we all waited expectantly for the key to turn. It did not! They continued right to the end of the alphabet and the key did not turn.

Tabitha said that meant she had not made up her mind yet. I was still skeptical, so they insisted that I try. Tabitha and I balanced the bow of the key on our fingers. The weight of the Bible was heavy.

To my dismay the key turned at E!

"Who do you know whose name begins with E?" Maria asked me.

"Elias Adams," Mama reminded her with a smile.

I objected strenuously as they teased me. I told them I would never get married at all.

Then Mama tried. Once again, the key did not turn. Mama laughed and said that was because she was already married. It was good to see her laugh. We have not been so light-hearted for a long time.

Then I suddenly remembered who else has a name which begins with E. Ellis! I had completely forgotten about him!

I do not think for one moment that I will marry Ellis. The key in the Bible is just a game, and it was simply a coincidence that it stopped at C for Maria and E for me.

But all the rest of the evening I have been thinking of Ellis. Is he still living in Government House? I remember staring at Fort Niagara, so close across the river. Is Ellis safe?

How I wish we had some news!

15 July 1812

Dear Constance,

Today we had a visitor! Old John Ball, the pedlar, knocked on our door. We were so glad to see him that we gave him tea and kept him talking a long time. We were surprised he was still making his rounds, but he said he has not seen or heard of any fighting on the Niagara peninsula. Mama was so relieved to hear that.

Mr. Ball told us that General Hull — he is the American general — crossed the Detroit River three days ago and took possession of Sandwich without bloodshed. I asked if Hamilton and Papa would have been there, but Mama assured me that Sandwich is far away from here and their regiment would not have been involved.

We almost forgot why the pedlar had come until he asked if we wanted to examine his wares. Mama bought ribbons, check fabric for aprons, white cotton stockings and a comb for each of us.

She told me that, now that I am nearing twelve, I may begin to grow my hair long. I prefer short hair but I suppose, if I am to put it up as Maria does now, I shall have to grow it. If only the rest of me would grow as well!

I am still plagued by mosquito bites. Mama asked John Ball for some ointment, but he had none. Tabitha tried covering me with a flour paste but I am still itchy.

I wish the pedlar had had more news. "No news is good news," Tabitha said, but how does she know that? And if there is no fighting in this vicinity, why cannot Hamilton and Papa come home to visit us?

16 July 1812

Dear Constance,

This evening after I brought back the cows I brought Mouse into the kitchen. Tabitha and I were amused to watch her play on the hearth, trying to attack a beetle. But then she began mewing for Patience and I had to take her back.

17 July 1812

Dear Constance,

Mama is teaching Maria and me a duet on the pianoforte. Neither of us is an accomplished player, and Mama sighed at the sound we produced. We so want to give her pleasure that we try not to blame each other for striking the wrong notes.

18 July 1812

Dear Constance,

We had another short letter from Papa, but once again it left out much more than it said. Mama says this is common during a war, that he would not be allowed to reveal to us what his regiment is doing. I was not at all comforted by her words.

I wish I could write to Hamilton and tell him

about the kittens. They play so strenuously, then they all suckle at the same time, then instantly collapse into sleep. Jack stuck his nose into the box and George tapped it! I think Mouse knows me — she staggered over when I called her name.

The wheat is almost ripe — it sways in the breeze like waves of gold. Mama is very worried about the harvest. How will we manage to do it by ourselves?

19 July 1812

Dear Constance,

Today was interesting for a change. Because I am so constantly itchy, Mama let Tabitha and me ride to the Twelve to get a root remedy from an Indian woman who lives there. She was reassured by John Ball's report that there is no fighting in this area. We promised to go no farther than the inn and to return within two hours.

How pleasant it was to go on a long ride again! It was very hot, but cool in the forest. Tabitha rode Hamilton's old mare, Bess. She is so fat and Sukie so stubborn that we could not go very fast. I gazed longingly at Abbie's farm when we passed it, but we did not have time to go in. To my great surprise, however, I spotted Mr. Seabrook pulling out a stump. He was too

99

far away to see us. Why is he here and not fighting like Papa and Hamilton?

We reached the inn and asked to see Mrs. Smith, whose husband works there. I asked her for roots for my bites. She looked at my red raised skin and shook her head with pity. Soon she had fetched me a package of roots, which she told us Mama was to boil, pound into a paste and apply to my skin. I gave her a length of ribbon in exchange. She was very pleased with it.

Usually there are many men coming and going at the inn — today it was deserted. But on the way home we passed a troop of soldiers on horses. The captain bowed to us. It was not Papa's regiment and I did not recognize anyone. I wonder where they have been and where they are going. Seeing them sent a chill through me — they are too real a reminder of the war.

Tonight Mama applied the root paste and my itching is much better.

20 July 1812

Dear Constance,

When I told Mama that Mr. Seabrook was home she was very surprised. She and Maria and I took the wagon to his farm to see if he could help us with the wheat harvest. Maria was as pleased as I was yesterday to have a change of scene.

We brought them a basket of cherries, some bread, a crock of maple syrup and some of our precious salt pork. How glad I was to see Abbie again! We whispered in a corner while the adults talked.

Mama has not visited the Seabrooks since Papa told her he disapproved of them — I wonder what he would think? Mrs. Seabrook was delighted to see us. She was very grateful for the food, as theirs has been humdrum. Raccoons ate many of their vegetables — they have been living on turnips and venison for weeks and long for something sweet.

Mrs. Seabrook is showing much more but feeling better than she did. Mama told her how worried she is about Caroline. The little boys climbed over Maria, who chased them and tickled them. We were having a cheerful time when Mr. Seabrook appeared.

He bowed to Mama but did not look pleased to have company. Then his wife showed him what we had brought and he became more civil. Mama boldly asked him why he was able to be here. He said that some of the militia were allowed to go home to tend to their farms. "And a good thing, too," he said angrily. "There is nothing happening in this absurd war."

We were relieved to hear this and eagerly asked

for news. He told us how General Hull had sent out a proclamation at Sandwich offering the American-born men in Upper Canada refuge in the States. "Many took advantage of this to go back to their former country," said Mr. Seabrook. "I do not blame them," he added defiantly.

Mama asked him if he had heard anything of Papa and Hamilton. He said he had seen Papa at a distance at Fort George. The men there are extremely bored, which is why some have been allowed home. There is a rumour that General Brock wants to be more offensive and directly attack the enemy, but he has been ordered to wait. "That is what your husband and son are doing — waiting for action," Mr. Seabrook told Mama.

"Let us pray they will not see it," said Mama quietly.

"But where is Hamilton?" I asked. "Have you seen him as well?" He shook his head, but assured me that he would be at Fort George with the rest of Papa's regiment.

Mama asked Mr. Seabrook if he could spare some time to help us harvest the wheat. He said that he would be finished with his small crop tomorrow and then he would come over.

I did not want to leave Abbie, but since the war appears to be at a standstill both our mothers said we could visit again.

21 July 1812

Dear Constance,

I do not want Mouse to become a wild barn cat — then I will never see her. I asked Mama if she could live in the house once she is weaned. "Hamilton would not approve," she started to say. Then she smiled and added, "But he is not here, so I give you my permission." I ran out to the barn to tell Mouse.

We are all greatly cheered by our visit to the Seabrooks. Mama is hopeful that we can cut at least some of the wheat. I am eager for Abbie to come here and meet Mouse. And we are very encouraged by the news that nothing is happening in the war. Perhaps it will end and everything will be as it was before.

My only regret is that Hamilton and Papa were not given leave as Mr. Seabrook was. I would so like to hear Hamilton tease me about Mouse.

23 July 1812

Dear Constance,

I am so weary I can hardly lift this pen. For two days we have been trying to save the wheat. What a time we have had!

We dressed in old clothes of Hamilton's — I

found some that he had as a child. I have never worn trousers before — how strange it felt, like wearing my pantalets without a petticoat to cover them! We started at six each morning.

Mr. Seabrook cradled the wheat. He is very strong and cut a wide swath, although he had a great deal of trouble with thistles. Tabitha and I walked behind him — he with his scythe, we with our rakes. My hands are blistered from twisting the stalks into a strand to bind the bundles. Mama and Maria stood the sheaves on end in stooks. After each hour we switched our duties. We stopped only for breakfast and dinner, and ended at six. It was so discouraging to have to stop! There was still so much to do and only us to do it — but by then we were too exhausted to work any more and fell into bed.

Then disaster struck. We had only harvested two acres when a sudden storm burst over us. The strong winds and beating rain flattened the rest of the wheat in minutes. Mr. Seabrook said it was ruined, since it would now start sprouting.

We quickly turned our efforts to bringing in the sheaves before they became any wetter. Frantically we piled them into the wagon and made trip after trip to the barn. The rain streamed from my hair and clothes, my hands were red and raw, and I truly thought my arms would fall off, they ached so. We did manage to save all the sheaves, however. They are piled in the attic of the barn, where they can dry safely until Hamilton is ready to thresh them this winter. (Will Hamilton be here to do that? How I hope so!)

I am proud of how hard I worked to save the wheat that Hamilton valued so highly. But the rest of the crop, much of my brother's whole 200 acres, is destroyed.

24 July 1812

Dear Constance,

Despite our great disappointment about the wheat I have had a delightful day, because Abbie's father brought her to visit. She was only allowed to stay for a few hours, but we had such a pleasant time playing with Mouse and pushing each other on the swing and jumping rope in the yard. Even Maria joined in.

I told Abbie how generous it was of her father to help us with the harvest. Indeed, I have greatly changed my mind about Mr. Seabrook. All the time we were working he was pleasant and kind, encouraging us when we were weary and praising us for how hard we worked. What I thought was harshness was simply reserve.

He told Mama he did not want to go back to

the war if the fighting starts again. They talked a lot about their homeland and how they hated having to regard it as an enemy. Mama told him about Aunt Isabel's family in South Carolina. The Seabrooks still have many relatives in Connecticut.

Mama said something which shocked me: "If the United States wishes to take over Upper Canada, why not let them? It is better to be one country and live in harmony, than to quarrel."

I am greatly confused. Which country do I belong to? Is the United States my homeland as well as Mama's? Papa (who would be very upset to hear Mama's words) would say I should be loyal to Britain. That is where, many many years ago, both his and Mama's families originally came from. Hamilton has already told me I belong to this new territory of Upper Canada, which seems so fragile at this time. Who is right?

25 July 1812

Dear Constance,

My life seems almost normal again. Today I rode over to visit Abbie after my chores. While she spun I took care of Paul and Johnny, but I did not mind. I am teaching Paul his letters and he is learning quickly.

The little time that Abbie and I are allowed alone we spend sitting in the shade under the large chestnut by the side of her house. We have been sewing a family of small dolls from scraps of material Mrs. Seabrook gave us. Tomorrow I will bring over some more.

This evening I brought Mouse upstairs and settled her in the clothes chest (with the lid open, of course). She was asleep when I put her in, and I was hoping she would stay that way while I wrote to you. But of course she started mewing and tried to climb out.

At first Maria objected to her being in the bedroom. But Mouse won her over with her antics and now she is curled up in the crook of Maria's arm. I will have to take her back to her mother before I go to bed, but in a few weeks she will be able to sleep with us every night

26 July 1812

Dear Constance,

Today I taught Paul how to write his name. How proud he was! He started writing it everywhere, in the dirt and on the door with a burnt stick.

Abbie and I continued to make our dolls. When she grows up she only wants to have one child, a girl, as she is so tired of looking after little boys. I would like to have six, three boys and three girls. I wish there were a way to have children without having to have a husband!

I made the mistake of telling Abbie about the divining game we played with the key and the Bible. Now she wants to try it, to see if the key turns at U. She has not seen Uriah since school ended and I am surprised she is still thinking of him. I told her the game did not really work, but she does not believe me.

27 July 1812

Dear Constance,

There was so much extra washing from our work cutting the wheat that I had no time to visit Abbie. I dressed up Jack in some of the soiled clothes, and Maria complained I was shirking. To get back at her I dropped a toad into her laundry tub. Mama scolded me sharply, but Maria's shriek was worth it.

28 July 1812

Dear Constance,

I am writing to you after supper. Hamilton and Papa are here! They have just gone out to shoot us a deer, so I will tell you about this exciting day so far.

I was sitting on the porch shelling peas before dinner when I saw two horses coming. When I realized who it was I jumped up so violently I spilt the peas. Papa lifted me high and Hamilton held me so close I had to protest that I could not breathe! Mama and Maria cried, and Tabitha's face was bright red as she got them something to eat.

As Papa has written, they have seen no fighting so far. Hamilton, however, has not been stationed at Fort George as Papa was, but has been in charge of a squadron patrolling the Niagara River. He greatly enjoyed the responsibility.

What a relief to have them safe at home, to see their faces and hear their voices! How refreshing to hear their news! It is as if we have been sealed in a dark room this past month and have finally been allowed to open the door.

They told us James and Charles are well, and that Caroline is staying with James's parents in Burlington. Mama was so relieved to hear that she would not be having her baby alone. Maria begged for more news of Charles, but there was nothing to add.

Tabitha came in and asked about Samuel. Papa told her he has not seen him since the war began. Later Tabitha told me how puzzled she is about this, since Samuel left for Fort George with Hamilton.

We were all chattering happily when the men made us sombre. Papa told us his regiment is about to go to Delaware Town, on the Grand River.

"I will be pleased to finally get a chance to fight," Hamilton said.

Mama responded by breaking into sobs and rushing from the room. Papa followed her.

"How could you say that, Hamilton?" Maria chided. "Can you not see how much you upset Mama?" Or me, I might have added, but I did not want Hamilton to think I was not being brave.

He apologized and instead began telling us about General Brock. "He is the greatest man I have ever met!" he said. "A real British gentleman, full of courage and energy. If anyone will persuade more men to fight, he is the fellow to do it." He has met Brock several times now and the General has even been to dinner at Papa's house.

I asked Hamilton if he had seen Ellis. "Who is Ellis?" he asked.

I explained that he is a boy who lives with General Brock. Hamilton said he had not noticed him.

"How do you know him, Susanna?" asked Maria. I told her I had met him at Fort George, careful not to mention our evening together.

I wonder if Ellis is still living in Niagara. If so, he must hear a lot about the war from the General. I imagine he worries about him as much as I worry about Hamilton and Papa.

Papa came downstairs and said Mama was calmer and resting. Maria and I then broke the news about the ruined harvest. The men immediately rode out to inspect the crops and came back looking grave.

Papa said he was sorry that he and Hamilton were not able to be relieved of their duties in time to come home. He praised us for our hard work and was thankful for Mr. Seabrook's help. "Perhaps I have been too hard on that man," he said, words I was very glad to hear. After admiring my blisters, he reminded us how lucky we are not to depend entirely on the farm for our living, since he receives a salary for being Sheriff.

Then Hamilton startled me. He said that he would give up farming and do something else after the war. Papa looked surprised, but said it was up to Hamilton, since he is in charge of the farm. I asked him what he would do. "Something more exciting than farming," he answered. How impetuous he is!

"Can we still live here?" I asked him fearfully. He assured me that we could. How I hope he will as well, and that everything will be as it was before!

I can hear the men coming in from their hunt,

so I must leave you and go down to savour every moment of my time with them.

Later

Papa and Hamilton are to leave very early in the morning before the rest of us get up. It is too soon! We all lingered in the parlour as long as we could, but now we have retired.

I brought in Mouse, and Hamilton teased me about befriending a barn cat. Then Mouse fell asleep on his lap! When I told him I was writing in this journal every day, he praised me for keeping up with it. Hamilton is writing regularly in his as well, and says we can compare them after the war.

I tried to smile as I kissed my dear father and brother goodbye. I am trying not to let my fears overwhelm me but already my tears are staining the page.

29 July 1812

Dear Constance,

Today at Abbie's I heard that Mr. Seabrook has been ordered to go back to his unit tomorrow. He is so angry that he does not speak. Their house is as heavy with sadness as ours.

How I despise this war!

Dear Constance,

I have been very ill with ague, which I get every summer. It is such a frustrating disease. One day I am feverish, then think I am better, then I am feverish again. I have been free of fever for a week, however, so I think it is over. I am very weak but am able to sit up during the day and can write to you.

Mama tended me, giving me constant sips of bark steeped in brandy. It always seems to cure me. At my worst I was so hot I could scarcely bear it. One night, Mama said, I did not know where I was but constantly cried for Hamilton.

On the days I felt better she sat by my bedside and told me stories about her girlhood in South Carolina. She had a Negro slave called Nan, of whom she was very fond. There are some slaves in Upper Canada who came here with their families, but their children are free at age five and twenty and their grandchildren free at birth.

I asked Mama if she thought that slavery was wrong.

She said that was a complex question. Her family was always kind to their slaves, yet she admits it is cruel to force people to work without pay.

It seems that the older I get the more complex

questions there are. Sometimes I wish I were younger and did not have to think about such issues.

As I got better Mama read to me from a book she borrowed from Mrs. Adams before the war, which Mrs. Adams's aunt had sent her from England. It is a novel called *Sense and Sensibility*. At first I thought there was too much about love in it, but soon I became completely engrossed. The people in it are so amusing and seem so real.

Maria and Tabitha came up to listen also, and I do believe it was wanting to know what happened next that got me through my illness. We only have the first two volumes, however, and I long to know the rest. The book has no named author, but is by "a lady." Whoever she is, I am full of wonder that she can write a story that seems so alive.

I wonder if I will ever love someone? I cannot imagine it, but it seems to be the major preoccupation of almost every adult I know. Perhaps I will not be able to escape it.

12 August 1812

Dear Constance,

Today I was able to go downstairs. I was overjoyed to see Mouse again, whom Mama did not allow in my bedroom when I was ill.

She is beginning to be weaned. I showed her how to lap milk by dipping my finger in it and encouraging her to lick it.

My legs are wobbly but my appetite is improving. I ate a large piece of rabbit pie for dinner.

Later

I forgot to tell you that while I was ill there was a letter from Papa. We have had a victory! It happened at Fort Michilimackinac on July 17. The Americans' fort is far to the north, in Michigan Territory, on an island in Lake Huron. Captain Charles Roberts defeated the Americans without bloodshed, with the help of his British officers, Canadian voyageurs and 400 Indian warriors. Papa said the American leader, Lieutenant Hanks, was so frightened of the warriors that he surrendered at once. We are lucky to have so many Indians as allies.

13 August 1812

Dear Constance,

I am much better and was allowed to go outside. Maria and I went for a walk. How delightful it was to feel the sun! I pushed off my bonnet and held up my face to it. Maria, however, made me pull it forward again. I do wish it were not considered unladylike to have colour on one's cheeks.

14 August 1812

Dear Constance,

This afternoon Mrs. Adams came to call! As there is still no fighting in this area she took the risk. She and Mama were delighted to see each other after so long. Mrs. Adams brought with her the third volume of *Sense and Sensibility*, which we are thrilled to have.

She also brought Elias. I was expected to entertain him while the others talked. After assuring Mama that I felt perfectly well, she let us go to the creek. We did not speak a word on the way — instead Elias blew a discordant tune on a willow whistle he had in his pocket. At least he did not taunt me as usual.

As we were throwing sticks for Jack, Elias grew friendlier. He told me how hard he has been working on their farm — just as we have. We boasted to each other about how much wheat we saved. He has not seen his father at all, and I felt sorry for him as I told him about Papa and Hamilton's visit.

"I wish I were old enough to fight the Americans," Elias told me.

"How can you say that?" I asked him. "Most of your friends are American!"

"Not any more," said Elias. "Anyone who lives in Upper Canada is part of the British Empire."

He does not seem to be confused about this war as I am. Perhaps that is because his parents have been here for longer than mine — they were some of the original Loyalists.

And how can he want to fight at all? I suppose, being a boy, he cannot help it. Despite his opinions, however, Elias is not quite as troublesome as I once thought.

15 August 1812

Dear Constance,

Mama let me ride over to see Abbie. Mr. Seabrook is still there! He refuses to go back, and Abbie is worried he will be arrested for desertion.

"Please do not tell anyone, especially your father," Abbie begged. Her face looked so pinched and anxious that I promised her I would not. I shudder to think of what Papa would think. But he is not here. Abbie is my closest friend and I cannot let her down.

I felt so confused that I could not talk about it any longer. Instead I told Abbie the story so far of *Sense and Sensibility* to cheer us both up.

The kittens are weaned and Patience is patient no longer. She walks away from them when they try to suck. Mama said that Mouse can now live inside. Right now she is purring at Maria's feet, waiting for me to come to bed. It will be so comforting to have her sleep with me all night.

I cannot decide if I should have made that promise to Abbie. I sympathize strongly with Mr. Seabrook. How can I not, when he feels the same way as Mama about fighting against his former country? Desertion is a serious offence, however.

I am so bewildered that I am not going to think about it.

16 August 1812

Dear Constance,

Every evening Mama reads to us from the last volume of *Sense and Sensibility*. It is so enthralling that I do not want it to end. I am used to just having the three of us again, almost as if Papa and Hamilton had not been here.

Mouse is now completely weaned and lives inside. Her brothers and sisters have begun to join the gang of barn cats, but Mouse sits on my lap in the parlour. It makes it difficult to stitch my sampler, as she is constantly pawing at the thread. I feed her milk and bits of meat. It is soothing to have someone to take care of.

17 August 1812

Dear Constance,

Wash-day again, so again I was not allowed to visit Abbie. Sometimes chores seem endless. Do you have to spend the whole day doing laundry the way we do, Constance?

Mouse caught a mouse in the kitchen. So she has proved her usefulness.

18 August 1812

Dear Constance,

Today Abbie and I were picking huckleberries when we met a bear! It was so close I could see into its beady eyes. Its face looked mild, but its glossy black body was so powerful and its paws so immense. I am used to bears, but they still send a shiver through me.

We made a lot of noise and it lumbered away. We dropped the pail of berries and had to fill it up again. Mrs. Seabrook was very pleased with how many we brought to her.

I passed Mr. Seabrook chopping a tree, but he turned his head when he saw me. I think he is avoiding me. Abbie and I do not speak of him. It is as if her father has become a ghost, someone who is not really here.

20 August 1812

Dear Constance,

I am in very low spirits. Today Mr. Seabrook took me aside and told me I should not visit Abbie any more. He is afraid I will tell Papa that he has not gone back to his unit.

I said that I had already promised Abbie I would not, and that Papa is not here anyway. Mr. Seabrook said, "I hope that you would not intentionally tell your father. But if he were here and he asked you directly where I was, I would not like you to have to lie to him. If you do not visit, you can honestly say you do not know if I am here."

He has brought back to the surface all the turmoil I was trying to suppress. Of course Papa should not know about Mr. Seabrook's desertion — he is the Sheriff! But I *would* find it difficult to lie to him.

In some ways I am relieved that Mr. Seabrook's decision does not force me to take a position. But how I will miss Abbie! Just when our life was beginning to seem normal again, our visits have to end.

And I do not know if Mr. Seabrook is right or not. Abbie says he will not go back for two reasons — he does not want to fight the inhabitants of his birthplace and, most of all, he does not want to leave his family, especially with a baby coming. Those are both reasons I can understand. Yet I know how much Papa would disapprove.

Who is right, Mr. Seabrook or Papa? Tonight I would like to pray that Abbie's father does not get caught. I also want to ask God to help us win this war so that it will be over — yet the war is against the country where Mr. Seabrook and Mama and I myself all have roots.

I wonder what God wants? I am so confused that I cannot pray at all.

21 August 1812

Dear Constance,

I would like to talk to Mama about Mr. Seabrook but I am afraid to. She admires him, but of course she would have to agree with Papa.

She asked me why I did not go to Abbie's when my chores were finished. I said Abbie was too busy for me to come. That is only half a lie, is it not? But how I hate having to lie to Mama at all.

This is too grown up a secret for me. It lies in me like a heavy weight and I wish I could be rid of it.

Dear Constance,

I helped Tabitha churn this afternoon. I have to stand on a stool to reach and my arms get very tired. But drinking the sweet buttermilk makes it worth the effort.

Tabitha is so distressed these days, worrying about Samuel. When Papa and Hamilton were here I tore a page out of this journal so she could send a letter with them. It is improper for her to write to Samuel when they are not betrothed, but she says she does not care. She hoped they could find him, but she has not heard a word.

I think she really loves Samuel now. She is so sad that I would give up her good company if she could be happy with him.

Mama asked why I was so quiet at supper. At least I could tell her truthfully that I was sad for Tabitha, even though that is only half the truth.

24 August 1812

Dear Constance,

I could not write yesterday because there was nothing to say. These are hot, dreary days and we are all out of sorts. Mama has one of her dreadful headaches. Maria is moping about Charles. After my chores I try to sew, but I cannot concentrate with all my own worries — about Papa and Hamilton's safety (we have had no letter since I was ill), about Mr. Seabrook, about Tabitha and Samuel. Last summer I had no worries whatsoever. I long for those tranquil days.

No one notices how often I let Jack in to lie under the table. Mouse snuggles between his paws. They are the only untroubled members of our family.

25 August 1812

Dear Constance,

We have used up almost all the deer that Papa and Hamilton shot. The salt pork is nearly gone as well. Mama is worried about what we will do for meat with no men to shoot for us.

Then Tabitha went out quietly and killed a chicken. I could not have done that. She says it was nothing, that she did it all the time when she was younger. We have never killed our chickens, but use them all for eggs.

It upset me to kill one of the hens I feed every day. I do not like to think which one it was. At least I have not named any more since I lost poor Snowflake.

This evening I was given the job of plucking

the hen in the yard. What a flurry of feathers! Mouse had a grand time pouncing after them. I spotted Wiggle and Blackie in the orchard and I was worried that Mouse would join them, but she seems content to stay close to me.

Mama keeps asking me why I do not visit Abbie. Finally I had to tell her we have had a quarrel. She tried to get me to say more, but I said I did not want to talk about it.

It pains me dreadfully to have to lie to her.

26 August 1812

Dear Constance,

General Brock came for tea! And Ellis! This day was so packed it is going to take a long time to tell you about it. I will try to write down every detail.

I was picking up the dry linen spread out on the bushes. A horse came up behind me so quietly that I scarcely noticed it until I turned around. It was a large grey horse, very handsome. Its tall rider was smiling. His musket and powder horn were slung at his side, and a clutch of dead pigeons was attached to his saddle.

"Is your mother at home?" the man asked me.

I did not know what to answer. What if this person were an enemy? I just stood there, my insides quivering.

Then the man told me not to be afraid, that he was a friend of my father's. "You must be Miss Susanna," he said. I curtseyed with great relief. If he knew my name he must be telling the truth.

Then he told me he was General Brock, and asked if he might come in to refresh himself. He said he had been hunting all day and had a great thirst.

I do not know how I stumbled into the house and cried to Mama and Maria that General Brock was here! They rushed out and Mama invited him in very graciously. She instructed Tabitha to pour him some water for washing and then to conduct him into the parlour.

She and Maria and I raced upstairs. Mama changed her cap and brushed my hair. She unlocked the tea chest she has hidden under her bed — in case of looting — and got out the precious souchong tea Hamilton had brought her. We hurried downstairs. Maria followed us shortly, dressed in her best muslin.

When General Brock stood he towered over us — he is well over six feet tall. I sat on my stool and gazed up at him. He was so busy admiring Maria that it was easy to do this without being rude. He has a large head, with fair thinning hair. His body gives the impression of immense strength. He has an English accent, of course, very clipped and precise. He was not wearing a uniform, but was dressed like any man who had been hunting.

We drank our tea and the General ate a piece of Tabitha's cherry pie. He gave us a message from Papa — he and Hamilton are safe and Papa is sorry he has not written for so long. They have been moving around too much to do so.

The General then told us about the great victory for the British at Detroit! General Hull surrendered and General Brock has proclaimed British rule over the whole Michigan territory.

Papa and Hamilton were not at Detroit. Papa had been guarding Fort George. As for Hamilton, he has been very brave! We hung onto General Brock's every word while he told us the story. He called Hamilton a very enterprising fellow, and told us that while he was near Delaware Town he met a group of American sympathizers. Hamilton and his men took possession of a house and pretended they were Yankees. The Americans revealed that they were also. So Hamilton took several prisoners and held them overnight!

General Brock went on to say that returning the prisoners to Fort George meant that Hamilton missed the Battle of Detroit. "Nevertheless I am well pleased with him," the General said.

How proud we were to hear that!

The General was obviously proud of his own victory too. It was partly achieved because he dressed the militia troops in red coats, so that General Hull would believe all of the soldiers were British regulars. General Brock gave equal credit, however, to the Shawnee chief, Tecumseh. Tecumseh had cleverly marched the same group of Indians three times across an opening in the woods. General Hull then thought there were two or three thousand of them, not mere hundreds, and immediately after, a white flag went up. The General said they could not have achieved such a surrender without Tecumseh. He called him a gallant warrior.

I listened to these tales of bluffing the enemy with great trepidation. War seems to be a great game, and to depend too much on luck. But what if these bluffs had not worked? Then Hamilton and General Brock and Tecumseh might not be alive! When the war began it seemed so distant. Listening to General Brock made it come right into our parlour.

The General said he hoped the Detroit victory would inspire more men to fight. He sighed as he spoke of how many deserters there were. I thought of Mr. Seabrook and squirmed with guilt.

Then he explained why he was able to take

time to go hunting. There is now an armistice for an indefinite period. General Brock's voice was angry as he spoke of it. I could see how impatient he was to keep on fighting and win.

"Enough talk of war," he said. He praised our large book collection, and he and Mama discussed how much they admired Homer. How cultured the General seems, how eagerly he spoke of literature and music! Maria sang for him — "Greensleeves," and she sang it with great charm. I am glad I did not have to perform as well, for I am sure my voice would have been worse than usual with nervousness.

General Brock turned to me and inquired how old I was. I said I would be twelve in October. It turns out that his birthday is the day before mine! He has two nieces about my age in England, to whom he sent furs to make into muffs.

I was already quivering with the thrill of having General Brock talk to me when I almost fell over with surprise — Tabitha showed Ellis into the room! He was white-faced and anxious, wiping his brow.

General Brock presented Ellis. He had been mending his horse's bridle. The General asked what had taken him so long.

Ellis bowed to Mama, then hung his head. "I

fear I got lost, sir. I found your directions confusing." The General laughed.

"Hello, Ellis," I said to him. "I am glad to see you again." Ellis smiled timidly.

Both Mama and the General looked surprised. We told them how we had met at Fort George in June.

"Ellis must be very hot," said Mama. "Take him into the kitchen, Susanna, and get him a cold drink."

We left the room and Tabitha poured Ellis a glass of spruce beer. Then she kindly said she would bring in the cows for me. Ellis and I could now talk freely. How delightful it was to see him again!

27 August 1812

Dear Constance,

Last night I had to stop writing, my hand was so sore. I have risen early to tell you the rest.

I asked Ellis about all he had been doing since June. He has had an even drearier time than I, with school let out and General Brock and his aides being seldom at the house. Porter took scarcely any notice of Ellis, apart from giving him his meals. Ellis spent long days by himself, reading or playing chess against an imaginary opponent. "Sometimes I walked to the fort, hoping for news of the General," he said. "But someone would always send me away."

Even when the General was home he was usually too busy to talk to Ellis. "I was very glad to come hunting with him today," he told me.

He looked so sad and lonely. "Are you not proud of General Brock's great victory?" I asked, trying to cheer him. "Surely Britain will win now and the war will be over!"

Ellis did not answer for a few moments and the expression on his face grew strange and distant, as if I were not in the room. "I do not know whether or not we will win," he said slowly. "But I have a great foreboding. Something terrible is going to happen. I do not know what it is, but I can feel its darkness."

His solemn words frightened me so much that I jumped up and took him outside. I introduced him to Jack and we walked around the orchard, picking the first ripe plums. Ellis acted normally again and scrambled up a tree. He actually laughed as the plum juice dripped down our faces and we tried to lick it off our noses.

"You are lucky, Susanna," he said suddenly.

I nodded sadly, thinking of the contrast between my happy, prosperous family, and this boy with no family at all. "I am very lucky and I am thankful for it," I told him.

"That is not what I mean," said Ellis. He looked into the air as if he could see something I could not. "I mean you are good luck. You bring luck to other people."

"What do you mean?" I asked. But Ellis would not answer.

He is certainly odd. Sometimes he seems much older than ten. But however peculiar he is, I like him even more than I did last time.

We saw General Brock come into the yard and Ellis ran to fetch their horses. General Brock handed me his pigeons "as a gift to your gracious mother," and I thanked him. I held his bridle as he mounted, and he told me that his horse is called Alfred. Then he and Ellis rode away.

We spent all evening talking about the General's visit. I will always remember that I have met a true hero. I wonder if I will ever see him again?

And will I ever see Ellis again? Perhaps when the war is over I will go back to Niagara and he will still be there. I do hope we can continue to be friends.

Later

If General Brock had asked me outright whether Mr. Seabrook was at his farm, would I have told him? I suppose I could have said "I do not know," since in truth I do not — although I suspect he is still there.

General Brock seemed so angry about the men who will not fight for him, as angry as he is about the armistice. He said that if he had enough men and was allowed to attack, he could win against the Americans right away.

I could feel his immense frustration and I felt sorry for him. Like Mama and Maria and Tabitha, I was completely won over by his charm. Yet I keep having to remind myself that the enemy he wants to vanquish is the country where I still have an aunt and uncle and cousins, the country Mama still misses so much, where Hamilton's future bride is now living.

This is such a confusing war.

28 August 1812

Dear Constance,

Today Maria and I went fishing. She has never gone before but Hamilton often used to take me with him. I found the crotched pole he uses and we took it with a large basket to the creek. At this time of year it is swarming with salmon. I showed Maria how to grab a fish out of the water with the pole and throw it to the bank. How she shrieked!

The salmon flapped about on the grass and I made Maria hold it still while I clubbed it dead with a stone. I do not like to kill such a beautiful creature. There are so many of them, however, I hope God understands that we need them.

At first Maria hated holding onto the flopping fish, but she soon got used to it. We caught three large salmon and then had to stop, for that was all we could carry. We arrived home soaking wet, covered with scales and blood. We were so filthy already that we proceeded to gut the salmon right away. I threw the entrails to Mouse.

Hamilton would be so proud of us.

Tabitha baked one of the salmon and we had part of it for dinner. It was delicious. I spent the rest of the day helping her smoke the rest. We now have enough fish for a long time.

This is the last of my pens. I keep trimming them but now they are stubs. I am also running out of ink.

Dear Constance,

I did not write to you yesterday because I have been busy making new pens and ink. As we keep no geese ourselves, Mama allowed me to ride to the Adamses' to gather some of their feathers. It is farther than going to Abbie's, but because General Brock said there was a cease-fire Mama decided it would be safe.

Elias helped me gather up feathers. He asked why I wanted them, so I told him about keeping this journal. I kept you a secret, Constance, because I know he would tease me about having an imaginary great-granddaughter. Elias said that writing sounded too much like school to him.

Like me, Elias was supposed to start school in Niagara next week — at the same school that Ellis attends. Because of the war, however, there will be no school at all. I am glad I do not have to leave the farm, but I will miss learning. Mama will not have much time to teach me.

I told Elias all about General Brock's visit and he was very envious of me. He also envied Ellis for knowing the General. "Papa thinks he is our greatest hope," he said.

When I got home I boiled the quills to make

them hard and pliable. Then Maria helped me cut them into pens. We made a dozen, but I still had no ink. Since the store in the Twelve is closed, there is no place to buy it. I decided to make my own.

This took some thought. I paced around the yard trying to think of something I could boil to make a strong colour and came up with — beets! After our usual Sunday service in the parlour I cooked down a great amount of beets. My hands are stained with bottling it. What do you think of it? It is rather weak and turns pink on the page, but it will have to do.

Mama says I am as inventive as Hamilton, which makes me proud.

31 August 1812

Dear Constance,

We are so tired of salmon that Tabitha decided to try to shoot some squirrels. I went with her and was surprised she knew how to load the rifle. She had never done it before, but had often observed Hamilton. Tabitha can do anything she sets her mind to! She let me try shooting but I disliked how painfully the gun recoiled against my shoulder.

After many misses Tabitha managed to shoot

three squirrels. I helped her skin them and we had them for dinner. They tasted somewhat like chicken. I am glad we did not have to kill any more real chickens. We need them for their eggs and I am fond of them.

While we walked in the forest Tabitha told me she is very anxious about Samuel. "Perhaps he is ill," she said. "Perhaps he died!"

I said that surely we would have heard from the Turneys if he had died. But would we? Samuel lived alone in a little house on the Turneys' property. Perhaps no one knew he worked for them. He has no relatives here — he came up alone from Pennsylvania.

I tried to comfort Tabitha but could find no words to reassure her.

1 September 1812

Dear Constance,

Mama is going to set me sums and lessons to do each morning. I must also read a book each week. I asked her if the first one could be *Sense and Sensibility* and she laughed and gave her permission. It is even better the second time, and I can hardly tear myself away from it. Maria is also supposed to read, but I predict that she will not.

2 September 1812

Dear Constance,

It has been raining heavily and I keep having to replace the containers we put out to catch the rainwater. Because I am trying to save the chickens, and because we are still having to eat our way through the salmon, I have set some snares for rabbits.

3 September 1812

Dear Constance,

I caught a rabbit! It pained me to lift its soft lifeless form, but if I get two more Tabitha will make rabbit pie, my favourite meal.

It rained all day.

4 September 1812

Dear Constance,

More rain. I caught two more rabbits, so I shall have my pie. Maria says I am turning into a boy, with all my fishing and snares. That made me cross at her, for I am only trying to help. Besides, she fishes also! We went again and came home with two more salmon.

5 September 1812

Dear Constance,

It rains and it rains. I get so muddy and wet when I take out the cows that I have to change my clothes afterwards. We ground the dried herbs and sealed them in crocks, then I worked on a shirt I am making for Hamilton. How I wish he could be here to try it on! Mama is teaching us whist, but I tire of it. She is very worried about Caroline, whose confinement is drawing near.

I miss Abbie so much and wonder what she is doing. Mama has given up asking why I do not visit her.

6 September 1812

Dear Constance,

As it was not raining for once, we made soft soap in the yard, even though it is Sunday. Mama says we have to do it while we can and that God would understand.

Tabitha added the lye to the grease in the cauldron, then we cooked it all day. I was given the job of checking the surface and adding more fat when it stopped looking greasy. Finally Mama put a dipperful in a saucer and declared it done, it now being a bright brown. We ladled the soap into tubs and pails and put it in the cellar to cool.

I am utterly dejected that all I have to write about is making soap.

7 September 1812

Dear Constance,

We received a letter from Papa, but there was nothing in it that we did not already know — all he wrote about was the Detroit victory and the armistice. If there is no fighting, why cannot he and Hamilton visit us again?

This morning we emptied all the cooled soap into a barrel. Tabitha keeps reminding me to give it a stir every time I pass it.

Then we had to make candles for the winter. It is very disagreeable to cut up the rancid animal fat and melt it down into tallow. Also, I got very tired of dipping the rods of strings into the tallow. I much prefer pouring the tallow into moulds, but Maria claimed that task.

We ended up with forty dozen candles. I will be glad to have them, now that it is getting too dark in the evening to write to you without one.

8 September 1812

Dear Constance,

Something very exciting has happened — Samuel is here! Early this morning I found him hiding in the barn, very tired and dirty, and dressed in ragged clothing. He asked me to fetch Tabitha. She was so shocked when I told her that she dropped the pan into the fire.

I sat in suspense at the kitchen table. Tabitha rushed in to get some bread and cheese to take to Samuel. After a long time she returned again.

She cautioned me to be silent as Mama and Maria came down to breakfast. Then I had to do my lessons, and then it was dinnertime. After it Tabitha took me aside and I heard the whole story.

Samuel ran away from the militia to New York State. He could have stayed there, but he returned to get Tabitha. He wants her to go back to New York with him and be married.

Tabitha is stunned by this, as am I. She will not tell me what she will do, but only begs me to keep Samuel a secret.

Will Tabitha leave us? I cannot bear it, yet I also want her to be happy. Thus I feel torn in two. If only they could be married and stay *here!* But then Samuel would be in as much danger of being caught as Mr. Seabrook. And of course, Papa would never allow it.

9 September 1812

Dear Constance,

Samuel is still hiding in the barn and Tabitha has still not told me what she will do. I am helping her take food to him. He is a shy man and ducks his head while he mumbles his thanks.

We spent all day picking beets, cucumbers, carrots and turnips, then packing them in barrels for the root cellar. Both Tabitha and I were so quiet that Mama asked us if we were ill. I *am* ill, with anxiety about Tabitha's decision. I long to ask her what it is, yet I do not, in fear of her answer.

10 September 1812

Dear Constance,

Samuel has left. Tabitha did not go with him. She told him she could not live in the country that is fighting her King, and could not leave us to cope in the war by ourselves. I am touched that she is so loyal to our family.

Tonight in the kitchen she put her head down on the table and wept for the first time since I have known her. All I could do was pat her shuddering shoulders in sympathy. I feel so grieved for her. Yet, selfishly, I am also relieved she is not to leave.

Perhaps Samuel will return after the war. We do not know if there is still an armistice, but perhaps that means the war will not last for long. I told these things to Tabitha but I could not cheer her.

11 September 1812

Dear Constance,
Tabitha goes through the day as calmly as if nothing has happened. She is so brave. Every morning, however, her eyes are red from weeping — she told Mama she has a cold.

We are bringing wood into the house to prepare for the cold weather. Thankfully, Hamilton has left us a large store of it. Tabitha taught me how to split kindling, but I am not strong enough to do it well. Mama says Maria must cut it instead. To my surprise, she did this without grumbling. The war is making her less lazy.

12 September 1812

Dear Constance,
All day we picked corn. My fingers are numb and my nose extremely sunburnt.

I am very cross with Maria because she tore a page out of this journal to write to Charles. I am more than halfway through it and every page is precious. I also worry that Maria has read it, although she assures me she has not. The only person I will allow to read this journal is Hamilton. If I think of him writing in *his* journal tonight, perhaps on a battlefield, I cannot help weeping a little.

13 September 1812

Dear Constance,

I cannot write down quickly enough what happened today.

Abbie came over! She was very hot when she arrived. After she had a drink I took her out to the swing.

She told me that her father's absence has been discovered! He has received a notice that if he does not pay a fine for deserting he will be arrested. The fine is twenty pounds.

"We do not have that much money!" Abbie sobbed. "Oh, poor Papa!"

She wept and wept. Mama came out to the well and asked what was the matter. Abbie could not help herself and told her everything.

Mama took her into the kitchen and washed her face. Then she told us to wait there. A few minutes later she came downstairs with a packet in her hand.

"Here is enough money, Abbie," she said.

"Have your father use it to pay the fine."

I gasped and asked her how she had her own money. She said she brought it with her from South Carolina years ago and has kept it hidden in her bedroom for an emergency.

Abbie could not believe her generosity. Mama said she was glad to help a fellow countryman. Then she solemnly made us promise never to tell Papa.

I took Abbie home on Sukie and left her at the top of their road. How fast she ran to show her parents the money! I went home slowly, full of bewilderment.

I am proud of what Mama has done. But she and Papa have always agreed on everything. He would be so angry if he knew and I would hate to see strife between them. I desperately hope he never finds out.

Tonight Mama took me aside and said we would never speak of this again. "It is something I had to do, but you are not to worry about it," she said. I kissed her, marvelling at her courage.

14 September 1812

Dear Constance,

Mr. Seabrook rode over to thank Mama for the money. He says he will start paying it back to her next year, when he sells his first wheat. Then he slaughtered some hogs for us. He also asked me to visit again any time I wished, so I will go tomorrow. I wonder if he will now return to the war?

Tabitha is still dejected. She never hums at her work as she used to and she does not tell us stories any more. Mama asked her what was wrong but Tabitha was silent.

Of course *I* could say nothing. So I have two heavy secrets, that of Tabitha and Samuel, and that of Mama giving the money to Mr. Seabrook.

15 September 1812

Dear Constance,

I spent all afternoon at Abbie's and did the usual things — helped her with her chores, entertained Paul and Johnny and worked on the dolls. Doing ordinary things is so precious.

We had a lot to catch up on since August. Abbie was full of awe as I told her about General Brock's visit and hiding Samuel. I did not tell her about Ellis. I am too worried she will tease me about him.

Abbie said a British soldier came this morning and Mr. Seabrook gave him Mama's money. If he had not, he would have had to go away with him. Now she thinks he is safe, because there is another furlough for all the men.

Does that mean that Papa and Hamilton will visit us again? Mr. Seabrook was swinging Paul and Johnny high in the air as I was leaving. Papa used to do that with me.

16 September 1812

Dear Constance,

Tonight I found that Maria had torn another page out of my journal! I was very angry and threatened to tell Mama. Then I said something cruel, which I regret. I told her it was not proper for her to write to Charles when they have no understanding.

Maria started weeping and said she knew she could not send the letters, but that it soothed her to write to Charles anyway. "It makes me feel I can talk to him," she sobbed. "And after the war perhaps we will have an understanding. Then I can give him what I wrote and he will know how much I missed him."

How I sympathize with that, Constance! Writing things down is soothing. I have gone through so many conflicting feelings since this war began. If I could not tell them to you I think I would burst.

Maria is so smitten with Charles and is so sure

that one day he will ask for her hand, that I could not be vexed with her any longer. I told her I would give her one blank page a week, and that she could use my pens and beet ink if she helped me to make more when they ran out. But I begged her to write as small as she could. It is impossible to get paper right now and I do not want to have to stop writing to you.

17 September 1812

Dear Constance,

Tonight I sat on the swing in the dusk. Jack was sleeping and Mouse slowly crept up on him, pouncing on his tail. He is so used to her he only wags it briefly. The cicadas were as loud as an orchestra and the fireflies swooped in the dark ening air. Pigeons cooed drowsily in the trees. The sunflowers I planted in the spring are taller than I am.

I never want to leave my home, and I pray that this wretched war will never destroy its peace.

18 September 1812

Dear Constance,

Tabitha has cheered up a bit. She says she will trust in God and pray that the end of the war brings Samuel back to her. Then she told me my favourite story, "Tom Tit Tot." It made me laugh so hard my stomach hurt.

I have finished all three volumes of *Sense and Sensibility* and I liked it even better the second time. I think I resemble sensible Elinor and that Maria is as foolish as Marianne. I told her this and she said *I* was foolish to say so. She was washing and I flicked water on her from the jug. We had a spirited water fight until Mama came in. She scolded us for getting damp and told us to go to bed.

19 September 1812

Dear Constance,

I asked Mama if she thought Papa and Hamilton would come home on leave. She said that because they were officers they probably could not get away. When I told her how much I missed them, she replied that she did too, and reminded me that we must all be brave.

I am so tired of having to be brave and cheerful! Sometimes I would like to shout out my rage at this war. But of course I cannot.

20 September 1812

Dear Constance,

The usual frustratingly short letter from Papa arrived, with no real news. The soldier who delivered it was David Putnam, who was in school with me three years ago. I tried to get him to tell me more about my father and brother but he just looked haughty and said, "I cannot tell you anything." How puffed up he was!

The weather is getting cooler and today I wore my flannel petticoat. We had roast pork for dinner and are very thankful to Mr. Seabrook.

Abbie and I have finished our family of dolls. There are five of them, a mother, father, girl, boy and baby. Each looks very handsome in the clothes we sewed.

Maria says I am spending too much time playing and should be doing my home sewing instead of sewing for dolls.

"You sound like Caroline," I told her.

That made her cross. "I only want you to help me with the new quilt," she answered. "It is not fair that I am working on it by myself."

I suppose she is right, but I do not have to listen to her. Unless Mama objects I will continue to spend time with Abbie.

21 September 1812

Dear Constance,

As well as our wheat, we are going to lose most of our apples, for there is no way for us to pick all of them. Every day we bring in as many baskets as we can manage, but most lie rotting on the ground.

Mama decided not to try to harvest the barley and rye, since even with Mr. Seabrook's help we would not be able to do much of it. This is a great worry — if the war goes on our food supply will be gone, and what will we do then?

I noticed that my dress was getting short so I measured myself on the door frame. I have finally grown — two whole inches! In sixteen days I will be twelve. Perhaps Papa will get me a horse for my birthday.

But of course Papa is not here and there is a war and my birthday has no importance.

22 September 1812

Dear Constance,

There is no time for lessons or sewing or playing with Abbie. We did nothing all day but make applesauce and apple cider. Mr. Seabrook came over in his wagon to fetch several baskets of apples we are giving them. He killed another pig for us and Maria and I caught some more salmon. Mama is proud of how well we have managed so far, but she is still worried about having enough food to last the winter.

23 September 1812

Dear Constance,

I helped Tabitha smoke some hams. Then I took a bucket into the forest and collected a honeycomb from a hive I found in the spring. The bees hovered around me but I wound a veil around my face and did not get stung.

When I have time to read I struggle with Foxe's *Book of Martyrs*, a very long book that Papa had as a boy. It is a history of the church with an account of the people who were martyred for it. I must admit I find it difficult and dry, especially after *Sense and Sensibility*.

24 September 1812

Dear Constance,

Mama told me I did not have to read the *Book of Martyrs* any longer, that I am too young for it. Instead I have begun her volume of Scott's poetry. When I come in from picking vegetables I snatch a few lines of it, which I enjoy very much.

The *Book of Martyrs* was one of Caroline's

favourites. We are thinking a lot of her, since her baby is due in a month. I deeply regret how thoughtless I was when she was here — I feel much older now. I miss her. How incredible it is that she will soon be a mother, and Maria and I aunts!

We pickled several barrels of onions and cucumbers. It is hard to believe winter is approaching, since the weather has turned warm again.

25 September 1812

Dear Constance,

We do not know if there is still an armistice — we never hear any news. But no news is good news, Mama says.

Abbie and I went for a long ride on Sukie, with Jack prancing beside us. The trees are changing to vibrant shades of red and orange. We talked about General Brock and Tecumseh. "Surely we will beat the Americans with these two heroes to lead us," I said.

"*I* am an American," Abbie reminded me sharply.

I could not reply. All my confusion came rushing back. I thought of Catherine, now in New York State, and how Hamilton, who loves her, has to fight her countrymen. I thought of how loyal Papa and Tabitha are to the King, how Mama helped Mr. Seabrook not to fight, and how Samuel returned to his own country.

Who am I loyal to? I do not know, and that is why I say again that this is a confusing war.

26 September 1812

Dear Constance,

I have nothing to tell you except that we have spent all day preserving fruit. I am also worried that I have used up well over half of this book, since I have had to sacrifice pages to Maria.

Thus I have decided that, despite my promise to Hamilton, I will only write when I have something important to say. The next time I see Hamilton — when, dear God, will that be? — I will ask him to get me another book.

6 October 1812

Dear Constance,

Today is General Isaac Brock's birthday, and tomorrow is mine. I am very low spirited, however, because no one has said anything about it. Perhaps they are meaning to surprise me. Perhaps Papa remembered the horse and is sending it tomorrow. But it is more than two weeks since we have heard from him at all.

Papa does not even know how much I have grown. He and Hamilton are probably too busy fighting to remember my birthday. I wonder if anyone has remembered General Brock's?

7 October 1812

Dear Constance,

I am trying to write calmly, to still my fear. Mama has left us. Early this morning James's brother, Peter, arrived in a wagon from Burlington. I have only met him once before, at Caroline and James's wedding. He is thirteen. He had driven all night to tell us that Caroline had the baby early and is gravely ill. Peter's mother is taking care of her but Caroline keeps asking for Mama and *she may not live*.

Peter had come to take Mama back to Burlington. It is a risk with the war on, but one she must take. She hurriedly packed and, after she and Peter had had breakfast, they left.

The baby is small but healthy — a girl, as yet unnamed. My niece! My happiness about that is cancelled by my misery about Caroline. How I wish I had loved her better! I keep thinking of how kind she used to be to me and I am once more ashamed that I played such a child-ish trick on her. I have not been a good sister to her and now I may lose her.

Before we retired tonight Maria and I knelt at the side of the bed and prayed a long time for Caroline. Now Maria is asleep but I got up again to write in here. Please God, make her better. Please God, keep Mama and Peter safe on their journey. Please God, help me to be brave. Mama told me to be brave when she left, but I do not know how much more courage I can squeeze out of myself. And there is so much to pray for, I do not know how God has time to listen to it all.

8 October 1812

Dear Constance,

I woke up this morning and remembered that yesterday I had turned twelve. I had completely forgotten and so, of course, had everyone else.

We have been wretched all day, going about our tasks dully and trying not to weep or worry. It is strange and frightening to be here with only Maria and Tabitha. This evening we huddled in the parlour and read the Bible. A wolf howled and we clutched each other with fear.

I can hear him again now. Perhaps it is the wolf I saw in the forest.

My tears are blotching the ink, so I will stop this and go to bed.

9 October 1812

Dear Constance,

A storm is raging outside. The wind is howling so much I fear the roof will come off. But we have a good fire going and Tabitha taught us a lively song, "King Arthur's Servants," which we sang as loud as we could against the wind and the driving rain.

I could not sing much, however, because I have a toothache. Tabitha has given me some feverfew tea to soothe it.

11 October 1812
Niagara

Dear Constance,

Yes, I am in Niagara! So much has happened that I can scarcely write fast enough to set it all down.

After a night of almost no sleep my toothache was much worse. My jaw felt as though it had a hot spike nailed through it. Tabitha said the tooth must be pulled. Maria held my head while Tabitha gripped with the pliers.

The harder she tugged the louder I screamed. Alas, she broke the crown! We were *all* crying as they gave me a dose of brandy.

As I lay moaning in bed Papa arrived! He smoothed my hair as he told us his news. Caroline is better! One of his men had been in Burlington and brought him the message. Papa had come home to tell us, knowing we were alone and how worried we would be. He said Mama would stay with Caroline until she was stronger, but she is definitely out of danger.

Papa now turned to the problem of what to do about me. He decided to take me to Niagara, so that the army surgeon could extract my tooth. As I watched Maria pack my small bag I managed to ask her to include this journal, a pen and a bottle of my beet ink.

We left immediately. Papa wrapped me in a blanket and held me in front of him as we galloped away. Mud flew in our faces and the jarring motion made me almost faint from pain. But Papa kept murmuring soothing words to me and I felt safe in his arms.

He rode straight to Fort George. Doctor Thorn gave me some more brandy and cut into my gum to twist out the tooth. I could hear it grinding against the bone and I almost gagged as hot blood gushed into my mouth. I gripped Papa's hand but still had to scream, splattering blood over both of us. I have never felt such pain and cannot bear to tell you any more about the dreadful experience, which I hope I will never have to repeat.

Papa then took me to his house, where I was put to bed. I slept until after dark. Then Hannah bathed me in front of the kitchen fire. What a sight I was, covered in blood and mud! Hannah was much less gruff than usual. She even called me a "poor little mite." I managed to sip a little soup and went back to sleep.

This morning I feel much better, although my jaw is very sore. Papa and Hamilton came into my room to kiss me before they left for the fort. How glad I was to see Hamilton again! I have just eaten a soft-boiled egg.

Later

Dear Constance,

I have spent the morning reading and wandering about the house. For a while I helped Hannah roll out pastry for a meat pie. Then I got bored and sat at the window.

The town is so changed from the last time I was here. Hardly anyone is in the streets. Hannah told me that many of the women and children have been sent away, but that she refused to leave.

I am so sleepy that I think I will have a nap.

The bed seems wide without Maria in it — it is the first time I can remember sleeping alone.

Later

I just saw Ellis! He was coming out of General Brock's house. I knocked on the window and he was so surprised when he saw who it was! I wish he had come to the house to say hello, but he just waved and hurried away. He looked anxious, as usual. I do hope I see him again.

Later

I have not seen Papa and Hamilton all day. Hannah went to bed early and made me go also, but I could not sleep. My mouth was almost free of pain and I had had such a long nap that I was not tired.

I watched at the window to see if I could spot Ellis again. I dozed in my chair, waking up twice because I fell off. First I heard Papa and Hamilton coming in very late. Then, even later, I heard a horse and watched General Brock dismount from Alfred and go into his house. He was shrouded in his cloak — it is raining hard again — and I could not see his face.

I lit a candle to write in here. I have just taken one more look out the window. The town is deathly quiet, except for the rain pounding down. It feels as if the world is holding its breath, as if something is about to happen.

October 13
Very Early

Dear Constance,

My fingers are quivering and you will probably not be able to read this shaky writing. Still, I must tell you what I have just done — perhaps the most important thing I have ever done in my life.

I was sleeping deeply and dreaming that I was being attacked by giant mosquitoes that buzzed and clattered around me. I woke up to realize that the clattering was something being thrown against my window. I ran over to it and Ellis was below, holding pebbles. It was not even quite dawn yet.

"Susanna!" he called, when I opened the window a crack. "Please come!" He ran back to his house.

I hesitated. What madness was this? It was still dark, the wind was howling and the rain thrashing. My bed was so warm. But I could not resist the desperate entreaty in Ellis's voice. I wrapped a shawl around my nightdress and put on my shoes. Then I slipped out of the house and knocked on General Brock's door, my heart pounding.

Ellis let me in and pulled me by the hand into the kitchen. He was very agitated, his eyes burning, his fiery hair in tufts, and his skin drained of colour.

General Brock was in the kitchen, putting on his uniform coat. Porter was handing him a cup of coffee.

Suddenly I was terrified. What was I doing here, disturbing this great man? I tried to leave before he noticed me, but he looked up and smiled.

The General asked me quietly what I was doing in Niagara — and in his house. I apologized, stuttering an explanation about my tooth. I said Ellis had asked me to come over but I did not know why.

Ellis looked at the floor. "I brought Susanna here to say goodbye," he mumbled.

The General was pulling on his boots. He gave Ellis a piercing look, then called him a strange boy. He *is* strange, I thought — why was it important that I say goodbye?

It was hard to believe General Brock was talking to us so calmly while obviously in a hurry to leave. I dared to ask where he was going. He said to Queenston, where they had begun fighting. "Can you not hear the guns?" he asked us.

I listened and, sure enough, there was a distant boom, muffled by the wind and rain. The sound made me shiver. General Brock told us he had not slept all night. "He who guards never sleeps!" he laughed.

His eyes were as fevered as Ellis's. The two of them were as tight with tension as wound up springs. At the same time the General's preparations seemed in slow motion, as if time had stopped.

General Brock tied a wide striped sash around his waist. He told us Tecumseh had given it to him. He put on his round hat. Then he stood up — what a giant he seemed! — and said these words: "Miss Susanna, would you buckle on my sword to bring me luck?"

I did not want to do it. I did not want him to put on his sword at all — that meant he would go off to fight and perhaps be killed. I was filled with a profound weariness of swords and battles, and of this war which has separated me from the people I love.

But how could I refuse? I glanced at Ellis, whose eyes were pleading. General Brock kept smiling at me and I had to give in. My great admiration for him won over my reluctance.

I nodded and he lifted me up to stand on a chair. Ellis handed me the sword in its ornate leather scabbard. As I was raising it General Brock said, "No, that sword will not do. Ellis, fetch me my other one."

Ellis ran out of the room and returned almost immediately with a long, curved sabre. He gave it to me, and my arms sagged under its weight. It was so much heavier than the first sword that Ellis had to help hold it in place while I fastened the stiff buckle. It only took a few minutes but it seemed more like hours.

General Brock thanked me and kissed me on the forehead. Then he lowered me to the floor. Porter handed him a dark cloak as he left the room.

We followed him out the front door. His aides, Macdonell and Glegg, were waiting for him outside. Alfred was harnessed and saddled and their own horses were ready. The General mounted and gave his aides some orders I did not entirely understand. But I heard him say that most of the troops were to stay at Fort George in case the battle in Queenston was only a distraction. That relieved me — perhaps Papa and Hamilton will not have to fight.

General Brock said goodbye and galloped into the windy darkness, his cloak flapping behind him. The two men got on their horses and rushed off to the fort. Ellis and I went into the hall to get out of the icy rain. For a few minutes we just stood there in silence. Ellis stared weirdly into the air, the way he had that day in our orchard.

"Why did you ask me to come here?" I asked, to break the spell he seemed to be under.

"I thought you would bring him luck," he mumbled. "It was my last hope. I told you before, Susanna — you are a lucky person. Even General Brock must have sensed it — that is why he asked you to buckle on his sword."

Then Ellis's voice choked. "But your luck is not enough. It will not be able to save him from his fate. We will never see him again."

I asked him how he could know that. "I do not *want* to know it!" he cried. "I just do!" He rushed up the stairs. I trudged back here, my heart full of dread and wonder.

I do not know what possesses that strange boy, but I pray that his premonition is wrong. *Please*, God, may my fulfilling General Brock's request bring him the luck he needs.

Later

We are now at Fort George. Hamilton woke us at six and told us that we had to take refuge in the fort. Hannah packed some blankets and food for us, grumbling at being disrupted.

Hamilton bundled us here in the wagon — Hannah and me and Ellis, who had been sent over by Porter in case the latter had to fight. I hurriedly packed this journal, a pen and some ink. Writing to you is all that keeps me calm.

When we reached the plain, we saw many troops assembled there. One at a time they were marching across it to the fort. A large group of Indian warriors was already heading to Queenston, their faces painted in red and black.

To my dismay, Hamilton told me that he and Papa were also to leave for Queenston at once. I clung to him so hard he had to pry me loose. He had tears in his eyes as he kissed me goodbye, but his eager expression chilled me. I wonder if I will ever see my beloved brother again.

We are shut up in the soldiers' barracks and not allowed to leave. Hannah is helping the women cook some gruel for breakfast. I was told to look after the little children. For a while I taught them cat's cradle with some lengths of string, but my heart is too heavy to amuse them for long.

It is dark in here and there is a strong smell of babies' napkins. I am sitting in a corner by a lantern writing this. Ellis is slouched beside me.

He will not eat or speak, but only sits and stares into the air with his haunted eyes.

Mid-morning

I am snatching a moment to tell you this, since I do not know when I will have the time to write again.

We were fired upon! When we heard the cannons Ellis and I raced to the upper floor of the barracks. From there we saw a horrifying sight. Smoke was pouring from the cannons at Fort Niagara and below us our gunners were firing back. I plugged my ears at the resounding booms. There are fires burning in town and I wonder if Papa's house has been hit.

To my terror, cannon balls were bouncing and smashing right here in the fort. Then we saw that a hot ball had set one of the storehouses on fire. "Come on!" cried Ellis. "We have to help!" He ran down the stairs. Fear held me back for only a few seconds — I could not let him go alone.

Hannah tried to stop me as I ran past her but I struggled out of her grasp and followed Ellis out the door of the barracks. Soldiers were passing buckets of water from hand to hand. Ellis and I joined the line. It took both of us to hold one bucket and I felt my arms were breaking, but our efforts won out and the building was saved.

Then someone shouted that the powder magazine had been hit! We ran over to see men on top of it, dousing the leaping flames. I cannot let myself think of what would have happened had the barrels of powder inside been ignited.

When both fires were out we stood behind the soldiers, trying to catch our breath. Ellis's face was grimy with soot and his eyes red with smoke, as mine must have been. My heart was pounding, but with exertion and exhilaration more than with fear.

Ellis pointed out Major General Sheaffe. We slunk behind a building to watch him, afraid someone would send us back to the barracks. The General was assembling a large troop of British soldiers. They quickly left the fort, I presume to join the battle at Queenston.

Ellis remarked on how stricken the General's face was, and said he must have had bad news.

"You are imagining things!" I told him angrily. It irks me how Ellis is so prone to think the worst.

Then an officer noticed us and ordered us back in here.

We can still hear the volley of cannons as our two forts fight one another. Children are whimpering with fright as their mothers try to soothe them. Hannah has scolded us roundly for going outside. She strictly forbids us to leave again.

Later

I am presently right in the middle of the war! It astounds me to write that, Constance. I have prayed for our safety. Yet I do not feel as frightened as when I was at home and the danger was invisible.

I keep thinking of General Brock's excitement as he got ready to leave, and of Hamilton's also. Is it the exhilaration that draws them to war, the same that still floods me from fighting the fires? I have never felt more alive than at this moment when I may be killed.

Later

Our brave General Brock is slain. The news has spread through the fort like the flames that were burning. All around me the women are gasping their disbelief. "What will we do now?" one just cried. "How will we win without him?"

When a soldier came in to announce it to us, Ellis did not cry out as I did. He only nodded, as if he knew all along. Now he is sitting against a wall with his head on his arms. I wrapped my shawl around him, as it is very cold in here. I wish I could comfort him, but he is far away from me. I am so sorry I was angry with him. He looks like such a small boy, huddled in his misery.

General Brock had already died when we were watching General Sheaffe, so Ellis was right.

As for me, I can scarcely absorb the news and can only pray that the same fate did not occur to Papa and Hamilton. I am ashamed that I wrote those words about feeling exhilarated. War is not about exhilaration — it is about death.

Evening

Hamilton and Papa are safe! I thank God for that. They arrived back at Fort George dirty and weary, but unharmed. The battle at Queenston Heights is over and we won, but at what cost?

I do not think that I have the spirit to tell you much more about the rest of this day. It was suffused with tragedy. By the early evening I could not bear to watch Ellis's lonely grief any longer. I wandered upstairs and gazed beyond the walls.

To my astonishment, hundreds and hundreds of American soldiers were being marched towards the fort. I quickly realized these were prisoners from the battle. As they drew closer I could see how weary the men were, and what an effort it was for them to march. Many were as young as Hamilton. They seemed ordinary, not like an enemy. They were someone's brothers and sons.

I wanted to get a closer look. Hannah was too busy helping to cook supper to notice when I slipped out the door of the barracks.

Then I wished I had not. As well as prisoners streaming into the fort, wounded soldiers had begun to arrive, some British but most American. Bodies were lined up in rows on the ground. Many were moaning with pain but some looked already dead. Many had gaping wounds. One had half his face missing, another his arm. Blood covered their uniforms and bandages and skin.

I scurried back to the barracks. I cannot write any more about what I saw, but its horror will stay with me forever.

Now I am beginning to believe that General Brock is dead. I keep hearing his kind voice as he asked me to buckle on his sword.

Why did I not bring him the luck he needed?

14 October 1812

Dear Constance,

Hannah and I are back in the house now. Papa has asked her to sew me a black dress for General

Brock's funeral, which is the day after tomorrow. There is a cease-fire, so it is safe for me to remain in Niagara for a few days longer. But all I want is to go home.

Several buildings were burned to the ground from the cannon fire, including the courthouse, which is next door. It is still smouldering and the air smells like charred wood. It could have been this house! Papa says he is glad we were safe in the fort, but I reminded him of the fires there. *Nowhere* is safe in a war.

Lieutenant Colonel John Macdonell, who fought bravely at General Brock's side, was seriously wounded. He was carried to Government House, where he died shortly after midnight. Now his body is lying in state along with General Brock's.

It is so hard to believe that their bodies are next door, when only yesterday morning I observed them both getting ready to fight. When I think of General Brock's height and vigour, of his kindness, I have to stop what I am doing and weep.

Hannah says I must learn to govern my feelings. She is still cross with me for leaving the barracks to help with the fire, and she is as exhausted as I am after our arduous time. This makes her even more disagreeable than usual. How I long for Mama!

I have to help Hannah sew my dress, but my eyes blur and I have to force the needle through the cloth. The house is very quiet. Papa and Hamilton are so busy getting ready for the funeral that we have not seen them since they brought us back here last night.

I wonder if Ellis is all right. What will become of him now that his guardian is dead?

Afternoon

I spent the morning doing more sewing until the dress was finally finished. It is very ugly and ill-fitting. Hannah is not a good sewer and, although I can make neat stitches, I am not any better than she at cutting out. I would have liked to go outside, but Hannah will not let me leave the house. Crowds of people walk up and down the street, all here for the funeral.

Hannah went to lie down and ordered me to do the same. But I could not sleep. My head was swirling with jangled images and sounds — the General's words, cannon fire, all those bleeding soldiers. I got up and discovered a copy of *Pilgrim's Progress* in Papa's study. For the rest of the afternoon I was immersed in it, and found it a welcome escape.

Evening

Hamilton stayed home after supper and we were finally able to talk. In fact, it was the longest I have had him to myself for months. I feasted my eyes on him the whole time, so glad he was alive.

We had so much to catch up on! First he described the battle. He and Papa reached Queenston just in time to hear about General Brock's death. The General led his men in a running charge up the Heights — I remembered how steep they were. His tall figure in his red coat made him an easy target. He had just raised his sword — that heavy sword I held — and turned to urge his men forward when he was shot in his chest.

Captain Glegg told Hamilton that General Brock's last words were, "My fall must not be noticed or impede my brave companions from advancing to victory." His body was quickly taken into a house in Queenston so the enemy would not know he was slain.

All of this was very difficult to listen to. Hamilton went on to tell me that it was the cries of the Iroquois warriors, led by the valiant Mohawk leader, John Norton, which drove off the Americans. So once again the Indians have helped us win a battle.

Both Hamilton and Papa played decisive roles. When General Sheaffe arrived he sent Hamilton galloping off to Chippewa for reinforcements. After the victory Papa was asked to help ride along the column of enemies and collect their swords, which he placed on the pommel of his saddle. Papa has been given the great honour of being a pallbearer tomorrow.

"Were you not afraid of being killed?" I asked my brother. He admitted to me that he was, that he thought of Catherine and wanted to live for her. But his eyes were still lit up with the flame of fighting. He would have gone over and over every detail had I not told him I could not bear to hear any more.

He asked me what it had been like being at the fort, so I told him how Ellis and I had helped put out the fire and watched the magazine being saved. "It was foolish of you to leave the barracks," Hamilton told me. "You are only children." Then he smiled. "But you were both very brave — I am proud of you."

I suppose we *were* brave — although I do not know if I would have done it without Ellis.

"You and Papa were braver," I said. "And General Brock." I stammered as I said it. I could not finish and tears filled my eyes.

"I hope that Father and I will always temper

our courage with good sense," said Hamilton. He smiled at me. "As I hope you will!"

He paused. "I will tell you something, Susanna, that perhaps I should not. General Brock was a very courageous man, but if he had not been so reckless perhaps he might still be alive. Do not tell Papa I said this, but I believe that gallant dash up the Heights was foolhardy. He should have ordered a captain to make the charge. But that was Brock's weakness, I think, his love of bold action — it was his Achilles' heel."

I shivered, suddenly remembering what Ellis had said. "Who was Achilles?" I asked. Hamilton explained how the mythological hero was invincible except for his heel, which was his downfall.

We both sat there silently, mourning our hero. Hamilton then caught me up with all he has been doing. When he related how he took the American prisoners, I said that General Brock had told us that when he came for tea.

"I knew he had visited. What a privilege for you to meet him!" said Hamilton.

I did not tell him I had met the General again. I did not tell him that I had buckled on his sword and that General Brock had kissed me on the forehead. I did not tell him about my great sadness and guilt that I am not "lucky" after all.

Why did I not relate all this to Hamilton? I think it was because I need to first sort out my churning feelings. They scour my insides like boiling water. I need to be quiet, to be at home and to ponder all that happened only yesterday morning. But I cannot go home yet, and here the war is too close for me to think clearly.

I believe these have been the two longest days of my life.

16 October 1812
Afternoon

Dear Constance,

I am going to tell you every detail of General Brock's funeral, because today I truly lived a moment in history. Writing about it also distracts me from my inner turmoil.

Hamilton and Papa had already left when I got up. My ugly dress itched me and was too tight under the arms. But that did not matter — at least I looked respectful. Hannah and I went out very early to get a good viewing place. Never have I seen such a crowd — there must have been thousands! Waves of people in mourning clothes spread over the streets like a black sea.

The procession began at ten. First came the red coats of the 41st Regiment, followed by the militia. As well as Hamilton, I spotted James and Charles and pointed them out to Hannah. Behind them was the regimental band, which played slow mournful music accompanied by drums muffled in black cloth. Every few minutes field guns were fired.

Alfred, tragically riderless and splendidly draped in ornamental coverings, was led by a groom. And then I saw Ellis. He was walking beside Porter, his face white and proud. He looked so small but his steps did not falter.

I recognized Doctor Thorn and Reverend Addison among the men who followed. Then came the caskets on gun wagons, first John Macdonell's, then General Brock's. Papa was marching beside the General's. I waved proudly, but of course he kept his eyes straight ahead. His left arm and his sword-knot, like all the other soldiers', were wrapped in black crape.

General Sheaffe looked so solemn. He is now our new leader. Hamilton said if it were not for his quick thinking the battle would have been lost.

General Brock's staff and friends followed his casket and we fell in behind along with the rest of the crowd. They pressed so closely and I could not see anything. Hannah held onto me firmly but I tugged and let my hand slip away as if by accident. I managed to wriggle my way through the crowd and find a clearer spot near the front of the procession.

The route to Fort George was lined with two rows of detachments, including Indians and the coloured troops in their green coats. All the soldiers held their muskets upside down. After the long procession the caskets stopped at the northernmost corner of the fort, at the Cavalier Bastion.

I squirmed to the front and was able to hear the whole service. Reverend Addison conducted it. When he said, "Earth to earth, ashes to ashes, dust to dust," I could not hold back my tears. A woman next to me gave me her handkerchief. The two caskets were lowered into a single grave, to lie there side by side. The grave was one of the casements Ellis had shown me in June.

After the internment there were three rounds of seven guns each. The Americans in Fort Niagara answered the salute and I could see from the fort that their flag, like ours, was at half-mast. It is a great tribute to the General that they honoured him as much as we did.

Everyone was grieving, but there was also a feeling of release, as if the war were over. But of course it is still here, like a crouching beast waiting to pounce on us again.

Evening

After supper, while everyone else was talking about the funeral, I slipped out and knocked on the door of Government House. Porter answered it and led me to Ellis.

Ellis was sitting in the kitchen, a plate of untouched food in front of him. The house was dark and gloomy, haunted by the tragedy that permeated it.

At first our words were strained. I told Ellis how well he looked walking in the procession. We talked a little about the funeral and he seemed to perk up in my presence, beginning to eat. I did not want to disturb him further, but I had to ask what was going to happen to him.

Ellis said that General Brock's will had provided for him, and that he was to be sent to school in England. I asked him if he wanted that. He shrugged.

"It is what General Brock wanted," he said, "and what my father wanted as well. I will try to like it for their sakes." His voice was sad but resigned.

Ellis cannot go to England with the war still on, of course, so until it is over he is to live with Porter in York.

There did not seem to be much to say after

that. I watched him finish his meal and then I said goodbye.

I will probably never see Ellis again. He is the bravest boy I have ever met.

17 October 1812

Dear Constance,

This morning Papa and Hamilton drove me home. Mama was there! I flew into her arms. Caroline and James and the baby were home as well. Caroline kissed me heartily and seemed in her old good spirits again. Perhaps it was just being with child that had made her so irritable. Even James was attentive to me.

"Come and meet your niece," Caroline said. The baby was sleeping in her cradle. She is a perfect small human with the tiniest fingers and toes. She is called Adelaide Margaret. I think those are fine names.

When she woke up I was allowed to hold her. I can help take care of her, for Caroline and Adelaide are to live here until the war is over.

We talked and talked, filling each other in on all that had happened. Maria was telling me so many things that my ears were ringing. She and Tabitha were very lonely with only the two of them here. While I was gone they had to fix a hole in the roof caused by the storm, and raccoons got into the corncrib.

Mama asked to see the space where my tooth was. It seems like years since my toothache, as if I were much younger then.

"Tell them what you did in the fort, Susanna," said Hamilton.

When I had finished Mama told me I was imprudent, but Papa said I was very courageous for eleven. I reminded him that I was now twelve.

"Twelve!" Mama cried. "Oh my dear child, how could we have forgotten?" Everyone looked ashamed and I assured them that it did not matter. Maria ran upstairs and came down with a needlecase in the shape of a small book that she had embroidered for me.

Then I told Papa how much I had grown. He took me on his knee and said he would have to do something about that. I scarcely dare to hope he knows my wish. Perhaps, at twelve, I am too old to sit on his knee, but tonight I did not care.

As we sat in the parlour I realized that this was the first time we have all been together since June. On Monday the men will have to leave us. But tonight, as Mouse purred on my lap, Jack slept at my feet, and my family chattered around me, I felt sheltered in safety.

18 October 1812

Dear Constance,

I am nearing the end of this book, but I must go back to writing to you regularly. Recording the daily routine of my life is the only thing that quiets the storm of emotions inside me. I shall try to make my handwriting tiny.

This morning Papa conducted a service of thanksgiving in the parlour. He thanked God for preserving the safety of the men in our family, for helping us win the battle of Queenston Heights, and for the heroic sacrifice of General Brock.

For dinner we had a roasted side of beef that Papa had brought home, with parsnips and green beans and pumpkin pie. In the afternoon I joined him and Hamilton in a ride around our land. I had to keep whipping Sukie to get her to keep up. Papa said, "I think you have outgrown that stubborn beast."

I was allowed to mind Adelaide for a whole hour while the others helped get supper. Her blue eyes stare curiously and she clenches my finger with great strength.

Charles rode all the way from Queenston to call on Maria. He told us that his sister, Mrs. Secord, had gone out to look for her husband on the battlefield at Queenston Heights. She found him wounded and dragged him home. What a brave woman she must be!

Mama allowed Charles and Maria to walk in the orchard. I was supposed to chaperone but Maria asked me to give them privacy, so I lingered under a tree. I have never seen Maria look so radiant.

After supper we played whist, and sang, and talked and talked. Our full house was suffused with contentment.

Why, then, do I feel such agitation? It is as if part of me is not really here, but still in Niagara. I have not caught up with myself since being in the kitchen with General Brock and Ellis, since listening to the cannons roar and seeing all those horribly wounded soldiers.

Papa's prayer made me even more unsettled. Did God want us to win? Did He *want* General Brock to be killed? Surely I should not have such thoughts, but I cannot help it.

19 October 1812
Morning

Dear Constance,

Last night in bed Maria told me that Charles has asked for her hand. They have to wait until she is older, but then they will be betrothed.

Maria gave Charles all the letters she wrote. She embraced me and thanked me for the paper. Then she made me promise not to tell anyone her secret.

Another secret! At least this is a happy one. I like Charles and hope he will be a steadying husband to my flighty sister.

Later

Papa, Hamilton and James left today. The truce has been extended, however, so they are going to try to come home again next Sunday.

I spent the day helping with the laundry and with Adelaide. I think she recognizes me. She is a good baby, rarely crying.

Tabitha asked me if I had seen General Brock before he was killed, since she knows he lived next door to Papa. I told her I had seen him enter his house that night. I could not tell her more.

20 October 1812

Dear Constance,

I saw Abbie for the first time since I have returned. We sat under our tree and she asked about everything that has happened. So I told her about my toothache, and putting out the fires in the fort, and General Brock's funeral. She was in awe of all I had witnessed.

Again, however, I could not unburden my great secret. I also still did not let her know about Ellis.

Abbie gave me a pretty green ribbon for my birthday. My hair is almost long enough to tie back. She is very happy because the cease-fire means her father does not have to worry about being called to fight for the moment.

She wanted to make more clothes for our dolls. I helped do so, but my heart was not in it. That game seems childish now and I feel older than Abbie, although I am not.

21 October 1812

Dear Constance,

Today I finally told Abbie about Ellis, how I had met him in June and seen him again in August and last week. Alas, her reaction was what I expected. She said that now that I had a boy I admired she could talk to me about Uriah.

"It is not *like* that!" I told her, but she did not understand.

22 October 1812

Dear Constance,

Now that Mama has Caroline to help with the household tasks she will have more time to teach me. This morning she came with me to the Sea-brooks' and asked if Abbie could join in my studies. They agreed that she could until the baby is born in January. I will be glad to have a companion in learning.

The weather is cold and every evening I heat up a stone to warm our bed. We hear Adelaide cry in the night, but she soon settles down after Caroline feeds her.

23 October 1812

Dear Constance,

This morning Abbie walked over and we had our first lesson together from Mama. She taught us some words in French, saying it would be useful for us to know some of that language if we ever went to Lower Canada. Mama had to stop us giggling and whispering, just as if she were a real teacher.

Despite how different I now feel from Abbie, she is still my closest friend and I hope she always will be.

24 October 1812

Dear Constance,

I took Sukie for a long ride in the forest. The trees are almost bare and there are many leaves on the ground. They look like bright coins strewn there. There was a heavy mist and when I saw someone approaching I could scarcely make out who it was.

It was Elias. He was taking a bag of wheat to his uncle's mill. I kept him sitting on his horse for a long time while I told him about my recent adventures. He was very envious that I had been in the midst of the cannon fire on Fort George. I wanted to tell him about how terrible it was to see the wounded men, but I could not bear to.

He would be even more envious if I told him about the sword. I almost did, but could not get out the words about that, either. Perhaps I will one day.

Elias said he admired how long my hair was growing. He was very friendly and I do not think he will ever plague me again.

25 October 1812

Dear Constance,

I have a horse! Papa and Hamilton and James arrived late last night. This morning, just as I was going out to collect the eggs, Papa put a blindfold over my eyes and led me to the barn.

There was a fine chestnut mare, wearing a handsome saddle and bridle! He lifted me onto her. I felt so high, but she is gentle and I can manage her easily. I am calling her Queen, after the battle. Her nose is as soft as velvet.

I have spent most of the day riding Queen — Mama has excused me from my chores, as if today were my real birthday. Once again we have a very full house. Papa and James have to return to Niagara on Tuesday, but Hamilton is to stay all week to shoot us some game, butcher some pigs and split some wood.

Queen is the best birthday present I have ever received. Having her settles slightly the agitation inside me.

26 October 1812

Dear Constance,

It is difficult to tell you what happened this evening. Papa was saying he hoped General Brock's gallant death would inspire more men to fight once the truce ends. "I hear Adam Seabrook was fined for deserting," he said. "Perhaps now he will be more loyal to Britain."

Mama asked him, in a steely voice I have never heard her use before, why Mr. Seabrook should have to fight against his own country if he chooses not to. And then she told Papa that she gave Mr. Seabrook the money to pay his fine.

The room was completely silent. Everyone stared at her in disbelief. My heart pounded, fearing Papa's reaction.

He asked Mama to repeat her words, and she did. Papa looked astounded. Then he said, "I greatly disapprove of your doing that, Polly, especially considering my position."

Mama said calmly that she was sorry he disagreed, but that she had done what she thought was right.

Papa got very red in the face. He asked Mama to come upstairs so they could discuss the issue in private. While they were gone we chattered nervously, playing with the baby and trying to pretend that Mama and Papa were not having the first quarrel I have ever known them to have.

Finally they returned. I glanced from one to the other as Maria and Caroline sang for us. Mama looked triumphant and Papa bewildered. I feel sorry for both of them, but most of all I am proud of Mama for standing up for her beliefs.

27 October 1812

Dear Constance,

I have at last been unburdened of my great secret. Hamilton and I went for a long ride, it being a fine sunny day. First he praised me for how well I handled Queen. Then he told me how much he missed Catherine and how he has not heard from her at all since she left. "I believe her father is forbidding her to answer my letters," he said bitterly.

While I consoled Hamilton, I worked up the courage to confide in him. Finally, as we rested our horses under a tree, I did.

Of course he was amazed to hear how I had gone into the General's house, how I had buckled on his sword and how General Brock had kissed me on the forehead.

"Susanna! What a great honour!" he said. "You will remember this the rest of your life!"

I nodded, but then I told him what has been tearing me apart — how futile my gesture was, how I did not bring General Brock luck at all. How futile this war is, when brave men like General Brock have to be killed, brave men like Mr. Seabrook and Samuel have to refuse to fight their own country, and brave women like Mama have to go against their husbands. I started to weep, telling him I did not know what to think about anything any more, even God — and especially this confusing war.

Hamilton got off his horse and lifted me down from Queen. He held me close until I stopped crying. "You do too *much* thinking for your age," he said finally. "Yes, it is a confusing war. So confusing that each individual, such as Mr. Seabrook and Mama, has to deal with it according to his or her conscience. Perhaps it is futile also — as all war is. I am already tired of it and I cannot see any end in sight."

He smiled. "As for God — how can *I* explain what He wants? It is our duty to believe that whatever happens is for our own good. Is this not what we learn from Scripture, that we have to put our trust in Him?"

"But what about General Brock? Surely his death was not for our own good! Was it God's will that he died?"

Hamilton sighed. "What difficult questions you ask, Susanna! Brock made his own choice. He took a great risk and it resulted in tragedy. All we can do — all God wants us to do — is to accept it."

This did not cheer me. But Hamilton went on to assure me that the General's death was certainly not *my* fault.

"But I did not bring him luck!" I cried. "Ellis said that I was a lucky person, but I am not!"

Hamilton told me that talking to me and having me buckle on his sword probably heartened General Brock greatly as he rode towards the battle. "And you bring *us* luck," he said, kissing my forehead. "This family would not be the same without your cheerful presence. My dear little sister, try to dismiss your worries. Be the happy child you were meant to be!"

A great lightness filled me. Perhaps Hamilton is right. It may be years before I sort out my feelings about this hateful war, before I answer all the questions, which plague me. Perhaps while I am still young I need not agonize about them quite so much.

I asked my brother not to tell anyone else my secret and he promised.

1 November 1812

Dear Constance,

Today being Sunday, Mama led us through prayers and readings in the parlour. The text today was "Trust in the Lord with all thine heart." It put me in mind of Hamilton's words yesterday. It also recalled to me Reverend Addison's sermon in June, about the tree being planted by water and having deep roots. I have decided I will use this text on my sampler.

This is the last time I can talk to you in this journal — I am on the last page and will have to write up the margins. Hamilton is going to bring me another book and some ink the next time he comes.

Once again we women are alone and once again we have no news. Perhaps the truce is over or perhaps the men are fighting again.

My life is full of not knowing. I do not know when this war will end, when Hamilton and Papa and James will return, or if my life will ever be as it was before. All I can do is trust that God will take care of us and will grant us peace instead of war.

At least I no longer have to write that I have no story of my own. I have looked danger in the eye and survived — as when I faced the wolf. You have read here, Constance, and can tell *your* ancestors, that I was part of history, that I once met a great hero and even buckled on his sword.

Epilogue

The war went on for two more years and became much worse for Susanna and her family. In May, 1813, the United States attacked Niagara and captured Fort George. They then occupied the Niagara Peninsula for six months. Charles Ingersoll's sister, Laura Secord, overheard the soldiers who were occupying her house in Queenston plan an attack on the British. She made a long, arduous and courageous journey by foot to warn the British officer, James FitzGibbon, who defeated the Americans at Beaver Dam in June. This, and the earlier Battle of Stoney Creek, drove the enemy back into Fort George.

Along with FitzGibbon, Hamilton Merritt also became a hero. Now the head of his father's regiment, he led raids against the groups of men who were traitors to Upper Canada, men headed by Joseph Willcocks, a personal enemy of the Merritts. The Niagara Peninsula became a kind of no-man's-land, where parties of British soldiers, Canadian militia, Indians from both sides and American troops stalked and fought one another. Two especially terrifying episodes for Susanna were when a group of the traitors looted their house for food, and when Willcocks arrived and took away Thomas Merritt, sending Susanna's father to the United States for a short time.

At the end of 1813 the town of Niagara was completely destroyed by the Americans. Its 400 inhabitants were given very short notice to get out of their dwellings. Hannah, who was alone, had to stand in a blizzard and watch Thomas Merritt's house burn to the ground. Thomas rode from Burlington, where he was stationed, to rescue her. Hannah, ill-tempered to the last, stayed with the Merritts as their housekeeper for the rest of her life. Although Niagara was rebuilt after the war, Thomas never lived there again, since he had by then retired as Sheriff.

In 1814 Hamilton was captured at the Battle of Lundy's Lane and imprisoned for the rest of the war in Massachusetts. There he met Catherine's father, who finally agreed to let the couple marry.

The Merritts' house was often occupied by British soldiers. Susanna disliked their arrogance and was desolate when they appropriated Queen for the war. She never got back her horse and bitterly resented it. Adam Seabrook managed to continue to evade fighting.

Everyone was relieved when the war finally ended. Hamilton returned home in March of

1815 with his new bride, Catherine. As he had planned, he stopped farming; he became a merchant, mill owner and eventual member of parliament. He was best known, however, for being instrumental in the construction of the Welland Canal between Lake Ontario and Lake Erie.

Tabitha had given up on Samuel, when he turned up unexpectedly in 1816 and asked her again to marry him. She did so on the condition that they stay in Upper Canada.

Caroline had another child, a son, in 1814. She and Adelaide were tragically drowned in the Niagara River in 1824. Maria married Charles in 1816; they had eight children.

Susanna married Elias Adams in 1823. They had one son, Thomas, and five daughters — Catherine, Sarah, Mary, Phoebe and Caroline. Sadly, both Thomas and Sarah died when only a few years old. Despite this great loss, Susanna enjoyed the busy social life in the rapidly growing town, now commonly called St. Catharines. Elias was one of its first mayors. Although Susanna never became the teacher she once wished to be, she took great pleasure in enriching her daughters' education. Abbie, who married Uriah and had seven beloved sons, remained Susanna's closest friend.

In 1851 Susanna read in the newspaper of a

lecture on the paranormal to be given in Toronto (the former York) by an Englishman named Ellis Babcock. She persuaded Elias to take her to the lecture.

Ellis spoke about methods of predicting the future. After the lecture Susanna introduced herself and her husband. Ellis was surprised and pleased to see Susanna, and she and Elias talked to him for a long time. He was now a professor of philosophy at Oxford and had written several books. He had never married, but seemed content being an academic. This was the last time Susanna ever saw him.

Susanna's parents, who had sold the farm and moved into the centre of town, lived into their eighties. Susanna herself, whose health was always precarious, died at age sixty-six. One of her greatest pleasures was to record her life in her diaries, which she kept in a locked wooden trunk. She survived long enough to give this trunk to Phoebe's daughter, Caroline, with instructions to one day pass it on to *her* daughter, if she had one. She asked Caroline to name this future daughter Constance, which Caroline did.

Historical Note

In 1791 the former Québec was divided into Upper and Lower Canada. Upper Canada (present-day Ontario) consisted of settlements along the upper St. Lawrence and the shores of the Great Lakes. It was populated by the many Loyalists who had fled north from the United States during and after the American Revolution. Upper Canada's first capital was Newark, later called by its original name of Niagara (and today known as Niagara-on-the-Lake). During the time that John Graves Simcoe, Upper Canada's first Lieutenant Governor, lived in Newark, the town was a thriving centre. In 1797 the capital was moved to York (now Toronto).

In 1812 Upper Canada had three main towns. Kingston, the largest, had a population of 1000, and Niagara and York each had around 600. Each of these towns had a fort manned by British soldiers. The rest of the province was populated by settlers whose main concern was establishing their farms in the heavily forested wilderness.

The population was a rich mixture: the British; the original Loyalists; "late Loyalists;" a constantly growing stream of immigrants from the United States, Britain and the rest of Europe; and the First Nations people. Although officially under British rule, sixty per cent of the population was American-born. Travel to and from the United States was common. Many settlers had relatives there, and dollars were used as often as pounds.

At the beginning of the nineteenth century Britain and France fought what were called the Napoleonic Wars. These conflicts ultimately led to the War of 1812 between the United States and Upper and Lower Canada. But why did Britain's fight with France spill over into North America?

Canada was part of the British Empire. The Americans, grateful for the support the French had given them during the American Revolution, were openly supporting Britain's foe, Napoleon. Also, the British were stopping American ships from trading with France, and sometimes even forcing American sailors into the British navy.

American land expansion into what was called "the Old Northwest" (south of Lake Erie and north of the Ohio River) was another reason for war. This was certainly the view of the "War Hawks" in the U.S. Congress, who believed that the British support of the native tribes already living there was hindering American settlers —

settlers who wanted to force the Indians to give up their lands.

The United States declared war on Britain in 1812. President James Madison thought it would be easy to take over Britain's colonies in North America. (Former President Thomas Jefferson had said it would be "a mere matter of marching.") The British and Canadians in Upper and Lower Canada were greatly outnumbered by the Americans, but better organized. Also, they had growing support from First Nations warriors, some of whom hoped that their involvement would result in the establishment of an Indian homeland in the Old Northwest. This was the ambition of the charismatic Shawnee chief, Tecumseh, who was killed at the battle of Moraviantown in southwestern Ontario in 1813.

Other tribes waited carefully before deciding which side they were on. The Iroquois on the Grand River, for example, were at first neutral, until their brave contribution to the Battle of Queenston Heights under the leadership of John Norton. In 1813, however, the Iroquois found themselves fighting against each other, which caused them to withdraw almost entirely from the war after the summer of 1814.

The war was fought on both land and water. It ended in a stalemate and is sometimes called "the war both sides won." The United States did not lose any territory, but if Canada had not fought off its American invaders it would not exist as it does today. The real losers were the tribes who had supported Tecumseh and played such a large role in the British victories. The negotiations after the Treaty of Ghent said nothing about the Indian homeland they hoped to retain.

Perhaps the most important result of the war was that it was the last time Canada and the United States ever fought. Since then the two countries have settled their disagreements peaceably and are proud to share "the longest undefended border in the world."

Because news travelled so slowly in the early 1800s, several events of the war were out of kilter with official timing. President Madison signed a declaration of war between the United States and Britain on June 18 of 1812, but General Brock did not hear about it until about a week later. When Lieutenant Porter Hanks was defeated by the British at Michilimackinac in July, he did not even know that war had been declared. The Treaty of Ghent was signed on December 24, 1814, but news of the war's end did not reach North America until February, 1815 — a month after the worst British defeat of the war at the Battle of New Orleans in

January. General Brock was knighted for his victory at Detroit on October 10, 1812, but he did not know of his knighthood at the time of his death.

For the rest of the nineteenth century the War of 1812 was overshadowed by the years-long fight against Napoleon. Only later did its heroes emerge: Laura Secord, whose famous journey now includes a mythical cow; James FitzGibbon and the daring "Green Tigers" regiment; inspiring and tragic Tecumseh; and Mohawk war chief John Norton (Teyoninhokarawen).

Dramatic events from the American perspective are the burning of the White House by the British (the scorched building had to be whitewashed, hence its name) and, in 1814, the penning of "The Star-Spangled Banner" (now the American national anthem) by Francis Scott Key during the bombardment of Fort McHenry at Baltimore.

Probably the greatest legends revolve around the figure of Sir Isaac Brock. The very British general, who often chafed at his time in Canada, is sometimes called a "Canadian" hero. His famous plumed hat has been depicted in paintings of him riding off to Queenston or ascending the Heights — but he did not receive this hat, which he had ordered in 1811 as part of his new uniform as a Major General, until after he died. (The hat is on display at the Niagara Historical Museum in Niagara-on-the-Lake.) There are several stories of Brock having been engaged to a woman called Sophie (or Susan) Shaw. He is supposed to have stopped by her house for a cup of coffee on his way to the Battle of Queenston Heights. The ghost of a weeping woman, "Sobbing Sophie," is said to haunt a house in Niagara-on-the Lake.

There are several versions of Brock's last words. One is that just before the charge up the Heights he said, "Take breath, boys — you will need it in a few moments." Other legends have him saying, "My fall must not be noticed or impede my brave companions from advancing to victory," or, more dramatically, "Push on, York volunteers!" (It is more likely that he died without saying anything.)

The glorification of the "Saviour of Upper Canada" grew to enormous proportions. In London, England, a memorial was soon created in St. Paul's Cathedral. In 1824 Brock's and Macdonell's remains were disinterred (Brock's features were apparently unchanged) and reburied during a second elaborate funeral at the site of the Battle of Queenston Heights. Shards from Brock's original coffin were distributed among the armed forces. One piece is now in Lundy's Lane Museum in Niagara Falls. The tower erected at Queenston Heights was partially ruined by a bomb in 1840. William Hamilton Merritt was part of the committee responsible for a second tower, the present magnificent structure, which was completed in 1856.

Brock's memory lives on. Numerous towns and cities have a Brock Street, and Elizabethtown, in Ontario, was renamed Brockville in 1812 in his honour. Brock University in St. Catharines also bears the General's name. No matter how exaggerated some of the stories about him, there is no doubt that Sir Isaac Brock's astute leadership and great courage sparked the defence of Upper Canada in the War of 1812. Without him, or another leader equally inspiring, the war might well have been lost.

The Niagara River at Queenston, showing the Hamilton house nearest the river. Robert Hamilton, whose family the Merritts visited, was a very important businessman and politician. His son George founded Hamilton, Ontario.

Although built later than the Merritts' house, this 1810 homestead in the Niagara region was probably similar to theirs.

The interior of Fort George, painted in 1804, shows the "lock step" marching style of the British infantry — and some tame bears!

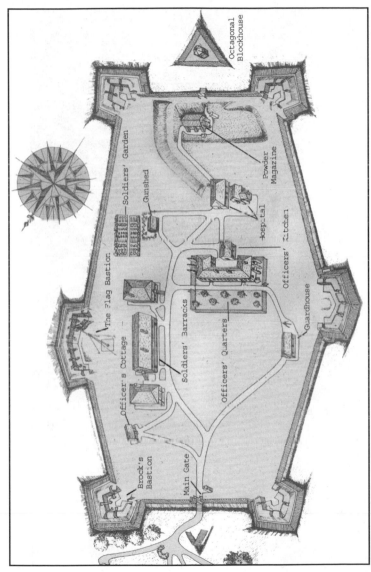

Octagonal Blockhouse

Powder Magazine

Soldiers' Garden

Gunshed

Hospital

Officers' Kitchen

The Flag Bastion

Guardhouse

Officer's Cottage

Soldiers' Barracks

Officers' Quarters

Brock's Bastion

Main Gate

A bird's-eye view of Fort George as it may have looked in 1812.

A view of the Horseshoe Falls in 1804.

Here's how to make a whirligig

You can make a whirligig like kids played with at Fort George. Find a large button and put a string through it like this.

Next, hold it like the boy in the picture. Swing it around to twist the string, then gently pull your hands apart. The whirligig will unwind, then wind up the other way. Can you keep it spinning?

To Make Syllabub Under the Cow

Put a bottle of strong Beer, and a Pint of Cyder into a Punch Bowl, and grate in a small Nutmeg. Sweeten it to your Taste, then milk as much Milk from the cow as will make a strong Froth, and the Ale look clear. Let it stand an Hour, then strew over it a few Currants, well washed, picked, and plumped before the Fire. Then send it to Table.

In this painting of Sir Isaac Brock he is wearing the "undress" coatee of a brigadier general, which he wore on the day of his death.

An artist's impression of Tecumseh. The courageous Shawnee chief was killed in 1813 at the battle of Moraviantown, one week less than a year after Brock's death. Tecumseh held his ground even though the British forces were defeated, and was slain.

The meeting of General Brock and Tecumseh. Brock called Tecumseh a "gallant warrior." Tecumseh is reputed to have to have said of Brock, "This is a man!" Here Tecumseh has been depicted more like a Sioux warrior than a Shawnee.

This print of the Battle of Queenston Heights combines several events at once, a common device at the time.

The famous painting showing the mortal wounding of General Brock.

The "coatee" worn by General Brock at Queenston Heights shows the fatal bullet hole, about level with the fourth button down. The striped sash is the one given to him by Tecumseh. Brock's coat and sash are on display at the Canadian War Museum in Ottawa.

A modern photograph of the powder magazine at Fort George, originally built in 1796.

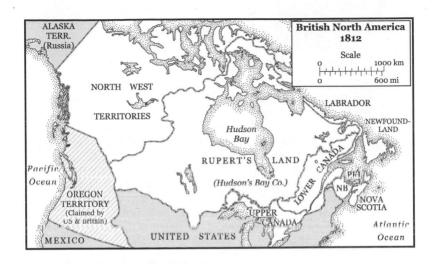

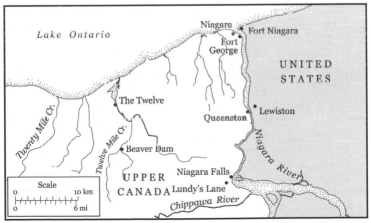

The area near Susanna's home at The Twelve, also known as St. Catharines. An important battle was fought in 1813 at Beaver Dam.

Acknowledgments

Grateful acknowledgment is made for permission to reprint the following:

Cover portrait: Detail from *The Little Knitter*, by William Bouguereau, courtesy of the Art Renewal Center: artrenewal.org
Cover background: John David Kelly, *Battle of Queenston Heights, 13 October 1812*, 1896 (detail, lightened), National Archives of Canada C-000273.
Page 205 (upper): Edward Walsh, *Queenston, or the landing between Lake Ontario & Lake Erie*, 1814; from No. 71, of Ackermann's Repository of Arts, National Archives of Canada C-003354.
Page 205 (lower): *Pen Pictures of Early Pioneer Life in Upper Canada*, by "A Canuck," published by William Briggs, 1905.
Page 206: James Walsh, *Fort George, Niagara River*, Clements Library, University of Michigan.
Page 207: Adapted from illustration by Barbara Bedell, from *Discover Fort George*, published by The Friends of Fort George.
Page 208: John Vanderlyn, *A View of the Western Branch of the Falls of Niagara, 1804*, National Archives of Canada C-014588.
Page 209 (upper): Whirligig illustration by Barbara Bedell, adapted from *Discover Fort George*, published by The Friends of Fort George.
Page 209 (lower): Recipe from *The Experienced English House Keeper* by Elizabeth Raffald, London, 1769.
Page 210 (upper:): John Wycliffe Lowes Forster (1850–1938), *Sir Isaac Brock*, National Archives of Canada C-007760.

Page 210 (lower): Imaginary portrait of Tecumseh, from "Tecumseh, a Drama," by Charles Mair, National Archives of Canada C-000319.

Page 211: Lorne K. Smith, *The Meeting of Brock and Tecumseh*, National Archives of Canada C-011052.

Page 212: James B. Dennis, *The Battle of Queenston Heights, October 18, 1813* [sic], ca. 1866, National Archives of Canada C-000276.

Page 213: John David Kelly, *Battle of Queenston Heights, 13 October 1812*, 1896, National Archives of Canada C-000273.

Page 214 (upper): Sir Isaac Brock's Coatee, AN19670070-009; copyright Canadian War Museum (C.W.M.).

Page 214 (lower): the powder magazine at Fort George, courtesy of Robert Malcomson.

Page 215. Maps by Paul Heersink/Paperglyphs. Map data © 2000 Government of Canada with permission from Natural Resources Canada.

Thanks to Barbara Hehner for her careful checking of the manuscript; to David Webb, Chief of Heritage Presentation, Niagara National Historic Sites of Canada; and to Susan Noakes of the Welland Historical Museum, for sharing their historical expertise.

217

For Ariel, Robin and Linnea,
true readers all.

Author's Note

When I started my first job as a children's librarian in St. Catharines, Ontario, my grandmother, Constance, told me that many of our ancestors came from there. That was when I became interested in the Merritts. At first I only knew about William Hamilton Merritt, who was famous for building the Welland Canal. Then I read, in a reminiscence written by Hamilton Merritt about his father, that his sister Susan had buckled on General Brock's sword for luck just before the Battle of Queenston Heights.

Susan Merritt was my great-great-great grandmother and this fictional story is based on her. In 1812 she was a year younger than Susanna. Her parents were what were called "late Loyalists," the second wave of Americans to arrive in Upper Canada after the Revolution. The more research I did, the more I was struck by how upsetting it must have been for Susan to be faced with the prospect of another war when her family had so recently fled from one.

The most exciting moment of my research was a tiny reference to General Brock having a ward, ₐ ten-year-old boy called Ellis. Now I had a way for Susanna to be with the General the morning of the battle.

Many of the family names and facts in this story are real, but others I made up. I hope any Merritt and Adams descendants whom I haven't met will forgive my liberties. Of course I have no way of knowing whether Susan's encounter with General Brock is true. Most likely it is a family myth, but it makes a wonderful story!

Kit Pearson is the author of six novels for children: *The Daring Game, A Handful of Time, The Sky Is Falling, The Lights Go On Again, Looking at the Moon!* and *Awake and Dreaming.* Kit has won numerous awards for her writing. She has twice been a winner of the CLA Book of the Year for Children Award and the Geoffrey Bilson Award for Historical Fiction. She has also won the Governor General's Award, the Mr. Christie's Book Award and the Ruth Schwartz Award.

Kit edited *This Land, A Cross-Country Anthology of Canadian Fiction for Young Readers.* She is a former librarian, and one of Canada's foremost writers for young people.

National Library of Canada Cataloguing in Publication Data

Pearson, Kit, 1947-
Whispers of war : the war of 1812 diary of Susanna Merritt

(Dear Canada)
ISBN 0-439-98836-5

1. Canada–History–War of 1812–Juvenile fiction.
I. Title. II. Series.

PS8581.E386W55 2002   jC813'.54   C2002-900299-0
PZ7.P32314Wi 2002

6 5 4 3   Printed in Canada   04 05

The display type was set in Galliard Book Italic.
The text was set in Binny Old Style.

Printed in Canada
First printing September 2002

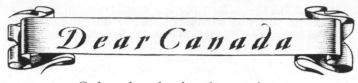

Dear Canada

Other books in the series: